Crossing The Line

Atlanta Edge Hockey

Carla Swafford

Acknowledgment

Thank you, Betty Bolté, for being a wonderful copy editor and friend. You can interrupt me any time.

Chapter 1

Kitty

"**C**ome here, Kitty!"

I scamper across the living room and bounce on the ottoman, landing on the sofa with my tail whipping back and forth.

"Meow!" I bunt my head against his chest. I love it when he tickles me beneath my chin.

"Quit," Roman says in his deep voice. His twinkling eyes tell me he's not mad. "We have thirty minutes before start of the Paws and Claws charity function." He pulls on my tail, scoops me up into his arms, and heads toward the garage door.

I'm five-one. So at six-foot-one, he has no problem carrying me without breaking out in a sweat.

Wearing a hound dog outfit with floppy ears, and a wolfish grin on his face, he's dressed perfectly, a perfect match to my kitty-cat costume. My hands lovingly roam over his biceps and he growls. I laugh and plant my palms on the sides of his face before pulling him down to kiss his blackened nose.

"Uh-oh. Did I get black stuff on my lips?"

He leans back. "Nope. Cute and pink." He swipes his tongue across my lips and up one cheek. I squeal, pretending to wipe off dog slobber.

His wicked grin warns me he will be doing that to me on and off all evening.

I can't stop my hands from wandering over his beautiful body. The costume's silky material clings to his muscles. His choice of being a canine is as natural as me being a feline. See, my name is Kitty. Actually, Kathleen, but as far back as I remember everyone has called me Kitty. He loves the name and gets a kick out of seeing other people's reactions when he calls me pussy, pretending to be innocently mistranslating Kitty.

He's a bit of a naughty joker. So I wasn't surprised the second week after I moved in, when he handed me a butt plug with a tail attached. I wear it and little else whenever he needs some cheering up. I like making him happy. I shrug with the thought. It makes me happy too. But for tonight, the tail for my costume is sewn to the back of my tights. The team's general manager and the coaches with their spouses will be at the party. No need to freak them out.

As Roman carries me to the door leading into the garage, I reach down and turn the knob.

"Thanks, doll."

I smile up at him as he steps out of the kitchen and then I pull the door closed behind us. We pass a dark blue Mercedes-Benz, one by a yellow Hummer, and stop next to a black Maserati in the middle of the huge space. My favorite of his six automobiles. The other three being a silver Lexus SUV, a red Silverado, and a stripped-down, green Jeep parked in a line on the other side. The Maserati is as sexy and savage as its owner. I've told him, he looks like a deadly *bratva* when he's behind the wheel. He likes teasing me about that.

Not only is he an enforcer for the Atlanta Edge, he's proven how truly dangerous he is through his stats. When the season ended for the team last week, sadly by losing to Nashville during the playoffs, he had over a hundred penalty minutes. He's a badass on the ice—a mean upper cut and all—and players dread to see the demonic gaze light up in his eyes when he's coming after them. They know once he delivers a body check, they'll be hurting the next day. What infuriates the other team even more is his mad puck skills. With over thirty goals for the season, he's a coach's dream. For some reason, Roman doesn't believe it. Every day, he works hard to improve.

I understood all of this even before I met Roman. I've loved hockey my entire life. My mom claims my dad played in the NHL though she refuses to tell me any more than that. I guess he hurt her when he left after finding out she was pregnant with me. Besides, she loves keeping secrets. I learned at a young age to take life as it comes and not to expect more than what those around me are willing to give. I think that's why Roman has let me stay with him for so long. His teammates have mentioned numerous times how he's kept me the longest of all his puck bunnies. I always smile and say I'm lucky that way.

With a sigh, I watch his long fingers smoothly turn the steering wheel as we back out of the garage and head down his long drive. Those strong fingers handle a car just as well as a hockey stick with such mastery. No wonder he does the same with my body.

The first few months we spent together, we had sex so much it's a wonder I can still walk. As the season continued —Roman played all of the eighty-plus games—our sex life tapered off out of necessity. He would come home, crash, and then he rose for practice and meetings before I opened an eye the next morning. Though without fail, before he left for another game or to meet a plane, he made sure I knew I was his.

The soreness between my legs, in my throat, and across my breasts tells me I still give him what he needs. But I still worry a little. I can only hope he's not losing interest. I try my best not to think about being told the fun is over and I must move on.

Only thing is I want to stay with him, to hold him, and hear his voice morning, noon, and night. I close my eyes for a few seconds to control my roiling emotions. He makes my heart flutter whenever I watch him stride into a room. He's special. He's fun, inventive, kind, and great in bed, but the man does not have a romantic bone in his body, and he's known for being the biggest tightwad.

Not that his money means anything to me. I've enjoyed being with him, living in his home, but I never expect money or jewelry or anything. Too many possessions only weigh down a person. But he does love to buy me sexy clothes, lingerie, and lots of sex toys. Really, do I need to say he's a bit freaky in bed? The aforementioned butt plug with tail? I'm okay with that. I love trying new things. And did I say the man was great in bed? Yeah. And it's not just because he has a cock to match his big, rock hard body.

"Okay, darlin', we're here."

Roman loves living in the Deep South and has picked up several southernisms and takes delight in dropping g's from endearments more than he should, what with his Russian accent. People misunderstand him so many times and tease him when he's excited and his accent becomes heavier, and he drops small words like *a* or *the*. I just think he's cute.

He gives me the eye and softly says a word in Russian. I understand. He's ordering me to remain in the car until he opens my door. Shivers of delight run down my body. His deep voice bossing me makes me feel protected and cared for.

I adore the sweet, old-fashioned things he does for me. He told me when he first came to the States, he practiced his English by watching old black-and-white films. A friend of his warned the newer movies had foul language, not appropriate to meeting American girls. Later, he realized his friend had teased him. He quickly discovered most of the women he met loved to hear those naughty words in bed and were not shy in repeating a few themselves. But he'd already fallen in love with the old American cinema. He still indulges in them whenever he relaxes during his time off. I've found I enjoy them too.

The car door opens and Roman holds out his hand. I smile up. The man may not be the prettiest man on the team, but I love those twinkling indigo eyes, broad shoulders, and big hands. The crooked grin with a chipped tooth at the top is so endearing. He's fortunate to have all his teeth considering most hockey players have one or more missing.

People in animal costumes of all types mill around the front door, waiting their turn to be introduced to the crowd. It's a charity event the majority of the team agreed to sponsor and attend. The no-kill humane society asked everyone to dress as their favorite animal.

My hand trembles in his as I follow him toward the entrance of the building.

"You nervous?" His accent is a little heavier than normal, showing he's apprehensive too.

"I'm meeting your coach for the first time." The team has several types of coaches, from assistant to goaltending, but I'm meeting one in particular face-to-face, and I don't know how to act or what to say. Guy McMillan, the team's head coach, doesn't go to just any party, and I've been to many given by Roman's teammates. Coach is known for his temper on the bench, though Roman swears the man stands cool in the locker room before and after games, winning or losing. He only lets the refs see his temper. He claims it helps them realize his seriousness about their idiotic calls. I will say the man is good-looking for an old man. Not that I'm interested—I'm over that sugar daddy phase—for I prefer men closer to my age. Anyway, he's happily married to his college sweetheart, and they have three smart and talented teenagers from what Roman has told me.

"They won't bite, especially Coach. Come on. Let's go. I'll protect you from the others."

"Didn't they say we had to be introduced so the media can take our pictures and place the right names on the captions?" Being such a savvy city, Atlanta's media still hasn't gotten their newest hockey team straight, distinguishing one hockey star from the next.

He ignores my comment about waiting his turn along with his teammates. The man is arrogant—with good reason as he's been MVP for the Edge his first two seasons—but I can tell he doesn't understand why people are saying to wait. Then again, being a hockey prodigy at the age of ten, he's used to people making allowances for him. So at times he forgets others' feelings.

"Roman." I tug at his hand. "Please wait."

With the smoothness he's known for on the ice, he turns and surrounds me with his arms. At last, we come to a standstill. I immediately forget the reason we stop as I soak in his heat and clean masculine scent. He smells so good. Though I can't say the same after a practice or game. The horrendous equipment odor...thank goodness, he always showers before I see him.

Being folded in his arms is heaven. Having this manly man holding me so gently is more than a girl can ask. I give a long sigh, and he chuckles.

"You are such *kotyonok*."

Kitten. He'd taught me that one. So sexy whenever he says it in Russian. His low, deep voice sends chill bumps along my skin, like now.

Smiling up into his dear face, I lift on my tiptoes and press a kiss to the little scar on his upper lip.

"I do enjoy rubbing against you." I purr each word and watch his eyes darken with desire. Yes. I can make the big man melt too.

"Okay, you two." Ryan Schmid, the Edge's captain and Roman's best friend, walks up and slaps Roman on the back. "The press keeps asking for when you'll get here. Let's get them happy so we can par-tee!"

Roman nods, places his hand at the small of my back, and we follow Ryan into the chaos.

For the next forty-five minutes I stand and hang. It's easy to get lost in the crowd. So many players, wives, girl-friends, puck bunnies, reporters, TV crews, celebrities wanting to rub shoulders with their favorite players, and then there is the poor staff trying to refill glasses and keep the tables loaded with food. I look over toward one end of the large room and see several animal cages the humane society brought, containing different pets who need homes. I don't dare check them out. I'll want one.

"Want to look?"

I jerk my head around to see who's reading my mind. A

beautiful blonde smiles at me. I know who she is. Mrs. McMillan. The head coach's wife. Slightly taller than me—that's not saying much as I'm short—with a little weight on her hips, she has the glow of a woman satisfied with life and happy to spread the joy. Nothing but good things are said about her from the other players and their dates. I still haven't met Roman's coach, but I'm in no hurry. I like to people watch.

"Look at the dogs?" I ask.

"We can. I thought you'll want to check out the cats. It's Kitty, right?"

I blink for a couple seconds. Wait. I'm dressed as a cat.

Glancing down at my costume, I smile. "I guess people would expect that."

She held out her hand. "Kitty Summerville, right?" Then I realize she does know my name.

"Uh, yes. How did you know?" Oh, goodness, I'm being rude. "Sorry. Yes. And you're Mrs. McMillan." I shake her hand. Her soft green eyes and smile are so engaging. I can imagine her husband adores her.

"Call me Millie."

"Millie. Okay." My smile spreads with the thought of calling her Millie McMillan. She has probably had many strangers commenting on the name alliteration.

"So you want to look at the dogs with me? I've been trying to convince Guy that we need one more pet. Our family pet died last year. Not that one animal can replace another, but we do miss how much fun they are to cuddle with when Guy is gone."

"I'm sorry to hear that." I've always heard losing a pet was like losing a family member, though I've never experienced it. My heart would break to have one and then for it to die.

"We worried Hannah, my daughter, would make all of us wear black until she recovered from the loss." With a teasing grin touched with sadness, she looks at me. "Thankfully, about that same time she met a boy at school, and he's eased her out of mourning. I have to say we all gave a sigh of relief, though Guy will argue with that. Fathers and their daughters. I guess you probably know about that."

I just nod and grin back at her. People who lived well-rounded lives with both parents never think others do not. They don't mean anything hateful by it, and I can't see any reason to take offense or make them feel uncomfortable by answering I never met mine. I'm certain my life was and is different from most people.

We walk slowly by the little pens filled with all sizes and shapes of dogs and cats. Millie picks up a little black-and-tan, long-haired puppy. From the size of the paws, it will grow to be a monster, but its big brown eyes pull at me. I keep my hands behind my back, twisting my fingers together. The house I live in is not my own. Having a dog is a big responsibility and I have no idea how Roman will react if I bring one home.

"Want to hold him? I think he's a German shepherd mix. Who knows what, with all this fur. He certainly is a charmer." She laughs and nuzzles the wiggling beauty.

"Oh, no you don't." A deep voice comes from over my shoulder, one I recognize from TV during interviews, causing me to jump. I turn, looking up. "Sorry to scare you," the man says with a rueful grin.

Guy McMillan is as handsome in real life as he is on the little screen. He looks different for he's laughing and hugging his wife. On interviews, he's always so serious and often glowers.

"Come on, Guy. It's not like we don't have the room.

Both of the boys will be out of the house soon." Millie dips her chin and bats her eyes.

"Yeah. You expect Hannah to feed and care for that monster?" He ruffles the bunched up fur at the dog's neck. The dog twists its neck and licks his hand.

I cover my mouth when I realize he agreed with what I thought about it being a monster. Not a terror, hopefully, but huge. The dog is cute. He's just so big.

"Kitty, help me here. Won't he be great as a watch dog while Guy's on his trips?"

My eyes go wide. Words refuse to come out of my open mouth. Millie has the wrong girl. I have no idea of what to say to help.

"Kitty?" Coach turns his attention to me.

Oh, no. What if he doesn't like me? Can he make Roman dump me? I don't want to leave yet. Inhaling deep, I steady my nerves. What am I thinking? Why will he care?

"Your name is Kitty?" He looks me up and down at my skintight costume.

From what I've already seen on the other women dressed as cats, mine is still conservative. Yet, the puzzled look on his face has me wondering, what does he see that bothers him?

"Yes. Kitty. I'm . . ." I didn't feel comfortable calling myself Roman's girlfriend and no way will I say fuck-buddy. He never introduces me in any way but as *this is Kitty*. "I'm here with Roman, Mr. McMillan."

He nods. "Nice to meet you. Call me Guy." He shakes my hand, none of the lingering touches or meaningful glances I receive at times. Thank goodness. Then he turns to his wife, and they begin to discuss the pros and cons of adding a new family member.

No way will I ever call him by his first name. He intimidates me like all get-out. I'm sure it has a lot to do with his being Roman's bench boss. While Millie has such friendly eyes and a forthright manner. I feel comfortable with her. Besides, I've learned at a young age if you call a man by his first name, he'll think it's okay to come on to you. I liked Millie too much to take that chance.

Feeling a little like an intruder, I take a step back and slowly ease away. When I twirl around to make my escape I slam into a tall, wiry body. I look up into Roman's agent's face. Casey Perry. The man does not like me. I don't know why. Every time I've been around him, he shoots me a look of disdain and loathing. When I first met him, I thought it was the way he felt about puck bunnies in general, but I've seen his reaction around other women dating hockey players, and he's all charm and smooth-talker and some of those players are his clients. It must be a natural chemical reaction or something I've done or said that I'm unaware of. So I stay away from him as much as possible.

"Hey, Casey. Sorry. I didn't see you there." Being Roman's agent, I feel it's necessary to be extra polite.

"It's Mr. Perry to you." He sneers.

"Oka-ay." I bite my lips, stopping the impulse to stick out my tongue, and nod as I look around in the hope Roman will walk up and save me from the awkward situation.

"Where is he?" His impatience is obvious in his sharp tone. He must be desperate to ask me about Roman.

I shrug and work on my fake smile. There are all types of people in the world a person has to deal with, no need to drop to their level. Keeping my mouth shut is best. It's not like the man can kick me out of Roman's life. Coach can get rid of Roman, and Roman can get rid of Casey. Actually, I think Roman can find a better agent. From what I heard from other players, the last contract should've been for a lot more. But Casey refused to play hardball with the Edge, telling Roman how lucky he was that the team still needs him with all the penalty minutes he drew. Like Roman missing out on the Maurice Richard Trophy the last three years by one goal each didn't mean anything. But what do I know about contracts?

"Stupid bitch," he mutters as he walks away. Unable to resist any longer, I stick my tongue at his back. He knew I can hear him.

Masculine laughter catches my attention. Standing off to the side, Mr. McMillan lifts his glass in salute before taking a sip. I blush. Before I can think of anything to say, he walks away.

Not a little embarrassed, but a lot, I walk away and wander around staying out of Mr. McMillan's way, stopping and saying a few words with a couple of girls who are always hanging with Roman's friends. Anything to pull my mind off getting caught being childishly rude. An hour or so goes by with no sign of Roman. I'm accustomed to being forgotten by Roman at functions like these. He always gets caught up in some tale or debate. The man is a social animal. Me? Not as much. I prefer hanging on the outskirts of the crowd and watching. Just knowing I'll be going home with Roman is enough. Besides, it's good for me to get out.

Another hour creeps along. I see Roman in a doorway that leads to smaller rooms where conversations are easier without shouting over the DJ music. Casey is laughing and talking as he shakes Roman's hand. Roman looks happy too. I'm glad. He needs something to cheer him up. I've done as much as I can without crippling myself showing how much I'm glad he's home for the next month. With his season cut short by the playoff loss, he hasn't mentioned anything about going back to Russia for the summer. From what he told me about his trip last year, it hadn't been the same after his mom's death the year earlier. His dad now lives in the U.S. with Roman's older brother and plans to visit after the hockey season ends, but that's all of his immediate family. He does keep in touch with a couple of aunts and uncles who visit and bring carloads of cousins. I've been told his dad, Sergei, is a cut up like his son, but his dad favors his other son, the doctor, over the one who plays a game for a living. His dad was a mathematician in Russia. So he thinks highly of jobs where you use more of the brain. I think it's sad he doesn't realize it takes more brains than brawn to play hockey and be a top-line player like Roman.

Someone bumps into me and I turn, smiling.

"Watch where you're standing." From the badge hanging around his neck proclaiming he's a member of the press, he gives me the once over, smirks, and walks on.

No surprise. They look at me as no one important. I can't argue with that. They know who the wives and long-term girlfriends are of the players.

Me? I'm only Roman's Kitty. I'm okay with that. No pressures, and I'm happier when it's just the two of us. He's charming and treats me so good. Sometimes he even asks for my opinion from movie plots to competing teams' rookies. I've never had a lover who ever asked my opinion on more than what color of tie to wear.

Maybe tonight I'll tell him how I feel, how I love him. I've never told anyone that before, but he's special. He'll probably laugh and say thank you. That's okay. People never take me seriously. Why should he?

I'm just Kitty.

Chapter 2

Roman

My body is buzzing as I fight the big, wide grin trying to spread across my face.

Does Kitty feel it? Probably. She loves touching me all over, even as I drive. Her caresses have my *khuy* stiff against my zipper and weeping. The woman makes me happy. She's affectionate, not clingy.

Like earlier tonight. I discussed some important business with Ryan, my friend and captain of the Edge, and then my agent. She stayed busy visiting with others while I concentrated on my future plans. I never have to worry about Kitty. She makes friends wherever she goes.

And now, I wait to hear from an old friend, Alexey Pulkkinen, a former coach of mine. The star forward on his team was injured during a big tournament being held in Russia. He'll know in a few hours if the forward can play the scheduled games over the next week or more. If not, I can replace him. This will be perfect for what I need.

There will be heavy scouting at the games, especially from NHL. Casey tells me I need to convince my current team, or another—I prefer one of the Original Six—to renew my contract for more than one paltry year, and as a center, not as a winger. My agent said they plan to place me on the third or fourth line this coming season. Sure, being in the bottom of the top fifty Maurice Richard Trophy contender list the last two years doesn't hurt. I'm in my prime at twenty-five, and given the chance, I know I can slam in forty or fifty goals. I've done everything they've asked. Now is the time for me to be in control. With the mostly positive attention from the last season, and depending on what medal I get playing in the tournament, my reputation will be set for life. I hate it for the injured player, but I have to take every opportunity given.

Excitement continues to vibrate through my body and much more. I glance down at Kitty. She's rubbing her cheek against my crotch, smiling up at me. Fuck. She's a hot, sweet girl. I do relish this dirty, submissive girl. I wish I could take her with me, but obtaining a Russian visa for a U.S. citizen takes longer than I have at this point. From what she's told me, she doesn't even have a passport. I want to tell her, but I don't want to jinx the chance of going. She'll be safe in my home for the short time I'll be away. Casey has my instructions if I find out favorable news this evening. I'll have to move fast.

I lift my hips and she unzips my pants. Like the wicked girl she is, Kitty dips in with her delicate hands and pulls me out, balls and all. Her mouth engulfs the tip and begins to lick and suck as she fondles my tight sac.

Yes. Life is good to me.

By the time I've driven into the garage and park, after almost running off the road as I come, she finishes me off and tucks me back into my pants and boxer briefs.

"You are so good with that talented little mouth. Come here." I pull her up and over my lap to kiss her. I'm impatient and want my tongue in her mouth. She tastes like sex and the champagne they served at the party.

Her body is soft in my arms and she purrs. I do love the sounds she makes.

I cup and squeeze her full tits. When I first met her, I was so happy to find they were real. I press and rotate the beautiful mounds, keeping a thumb on her hard nipples, flicking them with my nail. She catches her breath each time and presses harder against me.

"Please. Please. Let's go inside." My kitten is always hungry for me.

"You ready to fuck?"

She nods and grins, her eyes shining. She's so fucking cute. I've never met a woman so immersed in pleasing me.

My dick quivers as if reaching for her. I push the seat back and open the door, taking her with me. Her legs circle my waist and she grasps the back of my neck. Even as tiny as she is, I know she's sturdy and can take anything I dish out.

"Did you have to fight off other men at the party?" I whisper into her ear.

"No. They stayed away from me. They know this pussy belongs to you."

I groan when she says that. She gets me hard when she talks dirty, and I like knowing others are aware only I possess what she has.

In the time it takes to walk through the kitchen into the living room and up the stairs to my bedroom, I have pushed her thong and tights down past her ass and inserted a couple of fingers in what's mine. She's slick and ready for me. I drop her on her back, clasp the tights now at her ankles with one hand and hold her up, her ass off the bed. I slap one cheek and then the other over and over again to make them cherry red. She's squealing and moving her hips from side to side, but I know from our prior play she loves it.

When her bottom lands on the bed, I arrange her knees until they are near her tits and her pussy's wide open. The folds are soaked. One handed, I shove my underwear out of the way, I'm still unzipped, and take my hard, throbbing cock into my hand. With one hard thrust I'm in her and she's screaming my name. I do enjoy hearing it. I'm in control and she wants more. She raises her hips, meeting each thrust with one of her own. Her pussy tightens and releases around me. It never takes long for her to come after I spank her.

Time to make her come again. I keep pumping. I want to get my fill of her tonight. How can anyone compare to my little pussycat? I know this to be true, for whenever I go on road trips, I don't fuck other women. Strange how I hadn't thought much of that until now. Since I've met her, I hung out with my married teammates, those who were faithful to their wives, or I've been too tired to make the effort of bringing a puck bunny to my room. Hmm, that is odd. I've never been faithful to a woman before.

I pull out and with a clean jerk I discard her thong and tights including the tail onto the floor, and then shove her top over her head. I like looking at her. All bare, smooth, soft woman. My dick still thick, I dive back into her heat while I run my hands around her navel, over her sides, across her tits, and then her lips. Her dark eyes partially close. Her breathing comes fast and quick. Those pretty breasts moving up and down with each pant.

"You like me petting you, don't you, my little kitten?"

She arches her back as my hands cup her. "Yes. Yes. I like your big, rough hands on me."

"I like touching you too." Fisting a handful of hair at the

back of her skull, I bring her lips to mine. My tongue fills her mouth and then I suck on the tip of hers, causing her to moan. "I like especially how you let me do anything to you." I lick her bottom lip. The woman excites me more and more each day. Her sweet submission and game-for-anything attitude have kept me interested in her more than any puck bunny prior.

I reach over to the nightstand and pull out a tube of lube. Her eyes widen and become brighter. She knows what I want.

From the first time I spanked her, I discovered she occasionally savors pain while fucking. So a couple of months ago, I asked how she felt about anal. She gave me a crooked grin and shyly answered she'd never taken a cock as big as mine. Even though I was sad I wasn't her first there, I have to say our orgasms are explosive.

I pull out of her and flip her over. She automatically pulls her knees beneath her and raises her ass. I keep one hand between her legs and rub her clit. Without wasting time, I ease a finger on the other hand in the tight hole and work at stretching the little rosette.

"Relax, baby. Your man wants in."

She wiggles her butt.

I slap it. "Keep still. I know you want it as bad as I do."

Her moan tells me how much the preparation is exciting her. The woman loves to be dominated. Good thing as I'll always be in control.

The dark opening quickly loosens, even this part of Kitty is well-behaved. Carefully inserting the opening of the tube into her anus, I squeeze. Using my finger, I loosen the tight ring further and send more lube down the path my dick will follow. The anal canal does not naturally lubricate like her sweet pussy does. I don't want to damage her.

Once she's ready, I pull on a condom. Fuck, I prefer going bareback—we both have been tested and she has an IUD—and we do without in her pussy, but not here.

Pulling her warm, pink cheeks to the edge of the bed, I spread her ass and rest my dick in the crease, and then lean over to kiss her neck.

"You okay, Kitty?" I slide my hands beneath her to cover her tits and then tug at the stiff nipples.

"Oh, yes." She turns her face towards me. She's almost where she needs to be with my rubbing and tugging. Her dreamy smile is almost zen-like.

Standing straight beside the bed, I lift her hips and carefully nudge my dick into the tight opening. She's whimpering.

"Kitty?" I want to ensure she's still onboard.

"Please hurry. I need to come." She's becoming worked up with my slow stretching. She knows I'll spank her ass again and not in the fun way if she comes before me.

"You be a good girl, and I'll make you come hard again." Sinking into her, I groan as the narrow passageway grips me harder than any fist or pussy. My tip is in and I glide leisurely down with the lube. I draw back and pump back in, going faster with every thrust. She grunts with each lunge. "You feel so good. My sweet little *kiska*."

"You do too." Then she sighs when I pick up speed.

I'm about to come. No way can I last long in her tight ass. Grabbing a handful of hair, I pull and nip her earlobe and pinch a nipple with just the right pressure. She screams and orgasms for almost a full minute. I follow as I drill into her, feel the tightening and releasing from her lower body.

When I wrap my arms across her chest and my hands on her hips for a few seconds, I make sure not to give her my full weight.

"You're a good girl indeed. You make me very happy." That's when I hear my phone ring. "Fuck. Sorry. I must get that."

She gives a few murmurs of protest, but I kiss her temple and ease out. I grab my pants on the floor and toss her a hand towel from the supply in the nightstand. Then I head to the bathroom down the hall. She'll need the one in the bedroom to finish cleaning up. It's big enough for the both of us, but I want privacy. If my news is not good, I don't want her to hear and feel bad for me. I'll think of something else to help my career back on the right path, if that happens.

"Got good news for you, Volkov," Casey says without a greeting. My agent is happy I thought of this. He knows it can mean a higher commission for him with a new contract, and he didn't have to do jack shit. "Your contact called and said it's a go. I have your ticket waiting in the VIP lounge at Hartsfield, and they'll walk you through, but you need to be there soon. It'll take you an hour to get to the airport, and the plane will take off in less than three hours. By this time tomorrow, you can be practicing with the team."

"Good, good. I'll send you an email with final instructions about taking care of my Kitty. I'll tell her what to expect."

I dispose of the condom and rush through my shower. When I walk into my bedroom, my little kitten is sound asleep. All curled up with one hand resting on my pillow. Her sweet tush is light pink, almost back to normal. I'm tempted to wake her and tell her the news, but I notice the dark circles beneath her eyes. My big body wears her out. She's told me many times she gets her best sleep after my rough playing.

As I pack, I check on her several times. She hasn't

moved, but I know she's fine. Her lips are slightly turned up at the ends. She's having pleasant dreams.

Time is running out. I need to leave her a message. Sending an email from the airport would be simpler but she doesn't have email or any social media accounts. She's told me she didn't understand computers, and they hated her. I always laugh, thinking anyone or anything hating her is crazy.

So I do it the old fashion way. I scribble a note and hope she understands it. My writing is atrocious in Latin script as it is in Cyrillic. Leaving it by the bed, I lean over and kiss her cheek. I do wish I found a way to take her with me, but the time will fly by.

Inside I feel I'm forgetting something, but I can't imagine what it is. I shrug my shoulders. I know I can trust my agent to look out for my precious kitten.

Chapter 3

Kitty

"What do you mean get out?" I scramble to hold onto the mandarin orange I'm peeling as Roman's agent walks into the kitchen telling me I can't stay. I'm sure I misunderstood something.

"Pack up and hit the road." Casey leans, arms crossed, against the doorframe leading into the large family room.

Shortly after I woke up alone in Roman's bed, I took a few minutes to take care of things in the bathroom and then I went looking for Roman. He normally wakes me with kisses and snuggles, and tries to tempt me to take a shower with him. He usually wins. Or he'll be in the kitchen waiting with a massive cinnamon roll or a big bowl of sugary cereal in hand. The man loves junk food.

Instead the house is empty. At least, I thought it was until Casey scared ten years from my life when he showed up, telling me to get out.

"What did Roman say? Am I to meet him somewhere?" I feel my forehead wrinkle.

"You didn't read his note, did you?" The smirk on his face bothers me. "I knew you wouldn't."

"What note?"

He steps closer, giving me a once-over.

Whenever this man looks at me, I become skittish. Roman thinks a lot of his agent and trusts him. I don't have the same feelings. Casey's dislike of me can affect my relationship with Roman. It's important for me to get along with those who control his career. I don't want to embarrass or place Roman in a bad position. Besides, I'm easily replaceable, they are not.

"Roman asked me to do his dirty work. He's tired of you hanging around, spending his money. While he's in Russia, he wants me to dump out his trash." A smirk twists his lips as he crosses his arms over his chest and leans against the doorframe.

All the breath in my lungs leaves me. A cold chill runs over my face and down my body. What money? That doesn't make sense. Roman buys me stuff all the time without me saying a word.

"I don't believe you." I blink to stop the tears from falling. No way will I cry in front of this hateful man.

He straightens and moves a step toward me. "You stupid little girl. Do you see him here?"

"You said he's in Russia." I know he's taunting me, but my mind's racing, and I need time to piece this together. Something isn't right, but he won't stay quiet and let me think.

"He's not here, and did he ask you to go with him? No. He knew for months he was going and didn't say a word to you." He steps closer until he's towering over me.

I remember Roman telling me Casey had been a pro basketball player until a busted knee ended his career. The way he's eyeing me now, I don't like it one bit. I stand my ground. My pride refuses to back down.

My chest hurts with the thought of Roman keeping it from me. It doesn't make sense. If Roman didn't want me to go, he only needed to say so. There isn't a reason to hide it. If he wanted me out of the house, I would've been sad, but left without argument. It's his home, I have no claim. Nothing is adding up. Then again, my mom tells me I see only roses and sunshine.

He hovers over me like a vulture and then dips his head as if he plans to kiss me. I turn my head. A huff stirs the hair near my temple. He runs the back of his fingers down my cheek. "I'll be glad to keep you company while he's gone," he whispers in my ear.

Nausea washes over me. Throwing up on him will piss him off. Everything about his attitude and the way he normally talks to me warns of an ugly temper.

"You said I had to leave." I'm curious to hear what he'll say.

"As long as you're out before he returns, I won't tell if you don't." His hands grab my upper arms.

I jerk away and slam my fist into his junk. Being so short, it's easier to hit than knee him. He squeals and I run to the bedroom and slam the door, locking it and then pushing a chair under the doorknob. I'm not sure if it will hold, but it will slow him down enough to pack some things. If he calls the police, by the time they arrive, I'll be long gone.

I don't have much. I refuse to take the jewelry and expensive clothes Roman bought me. If Roman really told him to kick me out, I don't want him to think they mean something to me. I want Roman to see his wealth is not what kept me here. The only exception is one of the many Atlanta Edge blankets lying around. This one in particular we would snuggle under together, and it smelled like him. I inhale deep and sigh. Kissing it, I then spread it at the bottom of my old black backpack and place my clothes on top.

Despite what Casey says, I can't imagine Roman kicking me out in such a cold way. Believing that is the only reason I'm not sitting on the floor in a pool of tears.

Resting my ear to the door, I listen for Casey. Unless he's standing in the hallway, chances are I won't hear him in the huge house. The same about his inability to hear me. I grab my oversized purse and look around for what I'm forgetting. A picture of me and Roman sits on a dainty table he bought for me so I can see in a mirror while I apply makeup. The mirrors in the bathrooms were too far up to be comfortable. They were made for tall people like Roman. I sweep the picture and my makeup into the bag along with one of the many notes he's always writing to me.

It's probably the one Casey had mentioned.

Roman teases me endlessly about how I hate to read. So I tell him I find his voice to be sexy and prefer it over a piece of paper. Then he'll whisper dirty words in Russian and promptly translate as I melt into a puddle on his lap or on the floor, and before I know it, we're making love.

I carefully move the chair from beneath the knob and then crack open the door. The hallway's empty. I quickly tiptoe toward the back of the house. Within a minute I'm out a back door and dashing across the lawn into the apple orchard.

Roman said he bought the house for the beautiful blooms on the trees. He didn't know he had an orchard until he hired a lawn service and they told him. When it's time to harvest the fruit, he donates the apples to local missions and food banks.

About a mile from the house, I head toward the main

thoroughfare. I recognize several houses and know the direction I need to take to reach the highway that leads to my mom's house. Four hours later, I walk up her street and stand in front of her house. My feet hurt. My shoulders hurt. I hurt all over. About halfway, I had stopped at a convenience store and sat on the bench until the owner ran me off when he realized I didn't plan to buy anything.

The substantial one-level, brick house my mom owns is situated on a cul-de-sac and shares the half circle with the Phillips' larger plantation-style home. The Phillips are an older couple in their eighties. The two homes stand in an older upper-class neighborhood with big water oak trees lining the road. The whole area is peaceful with only the sounds of birds chirping in the branches.

After knocking and ringing the doorbell a couple of times, I walk around to the back and peek in a window. Her Cadillac sedan is gone from the spacious garage. I sit with a sigh at a little wrought iron table on her patio, so happy to get off my sore feet. The months of living with Roman have caused me to become soft, though he insists I exercise with him on occasion. Arranging the clothes-filled backpack on the table, I rest my head on top and wait. My whole body relaxes and I close my scratchy eyes.

"Kitty, what are you doing?"

I raise my head and blink. "Sorry, Mom." It's a habit to automatically apologize on hearing her voice. "I guess I fell asleep. It's so cool and quiet." The sun is going down behind the trees. The walk had certainly worn me out.

"Missy, you haven't answered me. Why are you here?" She stands in front of me with her hands on her plump hips.

A welcome every daughter wants from her mother. Not unexpected in this instance. She never minces her words with me.

Wait until she hears of Roman allegedly throwing me out. I don't trust Casey and anything he says. He always has given me the creeps. But I so dread telling her. Can I persuade her to ask me to stay? I almost laugh. The only time she asks me to visit is when she wants to impress someone, and she insists my boyfriend come along. Usually, the visitor is a big hockey fan.

"I just came to visit."

"With that large ugly bag? Unless you've lost your mind and brought your dirty laundry to wash," she says with horror in her voice. Her pale blonde hair—dyed to hide her gray, brushed from her face, and curled an inch above her shoulder—lifts in the light wind. Even with the fine lines around her eyes and mouth, she's still a pretty woman. "What have you done? You've caused him to be mad at you, and he kicked you out. You're not as young as you used to be and you've never been smart, so finding another man with his kind of money will be hard. What in the world were you thinking?"

"I'm twenty-four. That's not exactly old and decrepit." No way can I argue with the smart crack.

"But men don't want overused baggage. They like to think they have something different from what other men had before, if you know what I mean." Her southern belle tone gets haughtier with each word.

"Yes, Mom." I refuse to argue with her. Doesn't serve anyone any good. Only makes her madder, and I don't want to disturb the Phillips across the street, in case they hear Mom's shouting.

She releases a deep sigh and drops her hands. "Well, come on then. I have soup and crackers for supper. I might have enough to share."

My stomach growls at that moment and I blush. Luckily, she's already turned and headed toward the door. I creep along. My feet so tender, I tiptoe to avoid my heels. The fancy sneakers I wear didn't protect my feet like they claimed in the store.

The evening goes quickly, considering she barely talks to me and turns in at eight, giving me the stink eye when I mention watching a few minutes of TV. To keep the peace, I take a quick shower and crawl into the guest bed at the opposite end of the house. For about thirty minutes, I stare at the ceiling as I try to close my eyes and go to sleep with no luck.

Where is Roman? Probably his plane took off early this morning. He once told me it took over thirteen hours to arrive in Russia. How wonderful it would be to see the lights of Moscow or St. Petersburg at night. No. He's probably arriving in the morning there. To see the sun rise over the horizon on the other side of the world. That would be fascinating. He's told me amazing stories about the two cities and his childhood. Skating plays a large part in his tales.

Oh, I miss him. It has to be a misunderstanding. During my long walk I thought of nothing but what Casey said. Not once did he say how long Roman would be gone.

What a bad time to wish I had taken Roman up on the offer of a cell phone. I just felt funny about his spending so much money on me. What if I lost or broke it? It's doubtful I could operate it. Electronics confuse me.

I swallow and rub my eyes. The feeling of stupidity and loneliness washes over me.

Though I had been with Roman for months and met his teammates and their dates, I'm a little bit...well, okay...a lot of an introvert. Sure I talk with people if they start the conversation. To me, men are easier to be around. All I have to do is act interested and they talk my ears off. So, it had been by chance I met Roman.

My then boyfriend had just broken up with me by packing up my stuff and pointing me to the door of his condo. So today's event isn't unusual for me, but this is the first time a boyfriend's agent sent me on my way.

Like this morning, back then I had little to pack. Over that prior month, the man I was living with gave the usual signs he was bored with me. He stopped wanting sex, wouldn't talk, and often left me alone to go to meet his friends. So it was a relief to be told to go away. I wandered around downtown Nashville. With barely enough change on me to buy a meal, I stopped at a neighborhood sports bar and thought about where I could go and stay. At the time, Mom refused to arrange a way for me to return to Atlanta.

Over the years, I made a couple of female friends and spent a few nights with them while in-between boyfriends. For certain, women like me do not want another puck bunny in their house, and as time went by and being technology handicapped, I lost contact with them.

When it gets down to it, men baffle me. Between electronics and men, I guess I am a bit of a ditz.

I lived with the boyfriend before Roman less than three months, and at the time, it was my longest relationship in four years. I appear to bore men quickly. I had lived two years with my first boyfriend, and almost eighteen months with the second one. But since then, I've lost count of the number of men I've lived with. Some for a weekend and others for a few weeks. A couple were even gentlemen and didn't expect anything. I guess they felt sorry for me. Now the spaces in between were becoming longer. How depressing. I hate going to homeless shelters. Thankfully, I went to only one and that was enough.

The afternoon I met Roman in Nashville, I'd been sitting in a restaurant for a long time, nursing my soda and picking at a sandwich, wishing for a clue to what to do next.

Eight months ago...

The waitress stops twice to ask if I need anything else and I smile, and say no. It's the third time she's asked in fifteen minutes. I need to move on, but I still have no clue what to do. The thought of spending the night in an alley or a shelter terrifies me. I guess I feel sorry for myself. Tears well over and stream down my face.

A cool breeze and loud talking alert me to a group coming into the restaurant. I glance up and notice several tall, bearded men with a couple women in the mix. Looking away quickly, I wipe at my tears and try to pull myself together.

"Hey, beautiful. Don't cry. Boyfriend, right? I'll beat him up. Stupid man."

His deep accented voice brings a warmth to my soul. Every word comforts me and moves over my chilled body like a dark, sultry night. I know he's coming on to me, and I'm flattered.

Pretty is the most I've been called and I'm okay with it. But it feels good to hear a man say it.

"My boyfriend kicked me out of his house, and I'm trying to think of a place to stay."

I look over to the sexiest man I've ever spoken to in my life. Not exactly handsome, but good-looking in that masculine way athletic men have about them. He sat next to me, one arm resting on the booth cap behind my head and the other on the table, in essence blocking me in. He leans over. Even sitting down I can tell he's much taller. His broad shoulders and chest show he's a man who works out.

The only reason he doesn't scare me is his beautiful

blue eyes. He looks deep into mine. A kindness comes to them as if I'm a lost kitten in need of protecting. With a thumb, he wipes the wet trail from beneath my eyes and cups my cheek.

"Oh, my little one, do not cry. Roman is here to take care of you." Then he presses a kiss to my forehead.

It has been a long time since a man has treated me so tenderly and spoken in such a gentle tone.

"Thank you. It's been a rough day, and I'm so tired I can't think."

Those blue eyes stay on mine until he gives a slight nod as if coming to a decision.

"First, we eat. Then you come and stay with me."

He presses a finger to my mouth when I start to protest. I want to say no. Even serial killers can have kind eyes, I think. But I know who and what the man is. I've always been a big fan of the Atlanta Edge. Roman Volkov is known for his bold moves on the ice. Apparently, he thought nothing of being just as bold with his skates off.

"I have large house with five bedrooms. You pick any room to sleep in." A rueful tilt of his lips warn he's about to say something naughty. "If you pick mine, I can promise there will be no sleeping."

If I was a good girl, I would've blushed and said no and asked him to move away. But I'm not a good girl. And I'm a girl without a place to live, and the smile he gives me has my body tingling all over. A good feeling I have missed for a long time.

"Okay." I smile and kiss his cheek.

The beaming smile he returns almost blows my socks off, if I wore any.

He held his hand out. "Roman Volkov."

I reach out to shake, but he clasps my fingers and brings

them to his mouth, his lips lightly press the top. I lose my voice for a second and then cough out, "Kitty Summerville."

The naughty tilt of masculine lips again. "A sweet, little pussy. That's why you are so soft." He still holds my hand with his, while the fingers on his other lightly slides up my arm. Then he caresses my chin.

I almost purr.

"Who did you find, you lucky son of a bitch Russkie?" Another tall man slips in across from us. Compared to Roman's light chestnut hair, the stranger's is a deep red. His twinkling green eyes look from me to Roman and back. Then he winks.

"A sad little kitten, and I'm taking her home to tend to her." Roman quickly touches my nose with the tip of a finger and grins.

The man's eyebrows rose. "You do fast work." Then he looks at me. "Are you sure you trust this crazy man?" His accent is unlike Roman's.

"No. Do not scare her." Roman pulls me close to his side. "Do not listen to this batshit lunatic. He's only jealous because I saw you first."

"Seeing her first doesn't mean anything. She can change her mind now that I'm here." He leans across the table. "My name is Ryan Schmid. Don't trust this Russian. We Swiss are lovers not fighters. The country where they make all the delicious chocolate."

I laugh. Their humor relaxes me further.

"That and you have men in tights protecting the pope. Whoopee-do!" Roman squeezes me. "While Russians love to dance—"

Before he could say more, the stranger I recognize as the captain of the Atlanta Edge says, "Speaking of tights. Russians wear them too, but they jump around with their junk balled up in front so everyone thinks they have something to be proud of."

"Uncultured sheep herder," Roman says in his deep voice.

Laughing, I cover my mouth. I don't want to hurt their feelings. Their strange bickering makes no sense to me, but they are obviously enjoying it.

"Look. You have her thinking I'm as crazy as you." The man flashes a big grin, revealing the top two teeth in front are missing. Nothing unusual for a hockey player. Teeth being lost during a fight, high stick, or fall against the boards make it quite common. Probably the same reason for why Roman has a chipped tooth at the top near the small scar on his lip.

"Go, Schmidy. I don't want to see your ugly mug until practice." Roman jerks his head toward the crowd of lean healthy men. He places his arm around my shoulders.

Instead of getting angry, Ryan stands. "Nice meeting you, kitten." He gives me a sad dog look.

"Nice meeting you too." I bite my bottom lip to keep from laughing more.

Ryan slaps Roman on the back. "See you later, Lucky."

I wiggle. Roman's big body surrounds me like an electric blanket. Normally, I savor having a strong man hold me like this, but I need to look into his eyes. If he's lying, I hope I'll see it.

"Are you okay, little Kitty?" His husky accented voice stirs up all my senses. He smells like soap and man. Love it. His hand covers one of my hips, but stays in a safe zone. His other hand plays with my hair. I like that too. There is nothing about this man I don't like.

"I'm slightly warm. Can you move over an inch or so? Let the air in?" I need a little breathing room too. He overwhelms me in all types of good ways, but it will let me know if he can be trusted.

For a second, he doesn't move and then nods. A sexy smile comes to his well-defined lips. The small scar on his upper lip deserves to be licked. I wonder if another woman had kissed it all better whenever he received it.

"Sorry." He scoots over a tiny bit, but the air begins to circulate and I take in a deep breath. His gaze dips down to my chest but immediately comes back to my face. "What do you want to drink? To cool off?" He gives me a teasing grin I like a lot.

"I have this one." I pick up my glass and take a sip.

"Let me get us a cab and we'll pick up your belongings."

"I have them here." I point at the backpack next to me on the opposite side from him.

"A woman who comes prepared. I like it. Let me make a couple calls and we'll be all set." He turns to me with all kidding aside. "I promise, you will be safe with me. At any time you want to return here, I'll arrange tickets or a car to bring you back to Nashville. Good?"

Those blue eyes have such sincerity in them, I know he can be trusted.

Twenty-four hours later, I'm in Atlanta and inside his Lexus heading to his home. My head spins with how fast he moves.

Since Roman had to return on the team plane, and non-team members were not allowed on the flight, he arranged for a brother of another Edge player, to help me find my way through the airport along with getting on and off the plane. When I arrived in Atlanta, a security guard made certain I caught a taxi to the arena where the bus from the airport dropped off the Edge.

"Do you not have anyone you need to call and let them

know you're okay?" He glances my way as he handles the steering wheel like an expert.

"Not really. My mom lives here but we don't talk much." I look at him, biting one side of my bottom lip. "I guess I'll have to depend on you being a good person." The men in my life have been people who I associated with through previous boyfriends or acquaintances. The hockey world is a close-knit group, and little can be kept secret. I've never heard anything negative about Roman and his personal life, but you never know.

He grunts and pulls into a gated community and then onto a lengthy driveway.

As soon as we pull into the fifth bay of a six-bay garage, he turns off the engine. He faces me and cups my cheek.

"Kitty, nothing to fear. You stay. In a week, I go on the road. So you have the house to yourself. If you need anything, just ask. You will be safe here. I expect nothing." He chuckles. "Your expression tells me you think I lie. You'll see."

"I've never met a man who didn't want something more. So what do you expect from me?" The way his eyes flash hot, I know I'm right. I like how he burns for me too.

He smooths my hair from my forehead. "I am a man and you are a sexy woman. But anytime you wish to leave, I will get you hotel room and help you. If you like me and my place and want to hang with me. That be good. We will take one day at a time. All your decision."

His husky, accented voice curls my toes and heats my blood even hotter. I slip my arms around his neck and lift up to reach his lips. I've been watching his mouth all evening, wanting to kiss him, to discover how he tastes. He kisses me like a man needing substance, and I'm the only one to provide it.

I lean away enough to lick his bottom lip. He groans.

"My little *kiska*." He pulls me across the console into his lap. "I like you licking me. That tasty mouth probably has many tricks. Maybe I will test it soon, but tonight," his regretful look almost brings a giggle from me, he really is a charmer, "your eyes tell me you are tired as I am."

"I'm a little. It's been a rollercoaster of a day."

"Nashville has one like Six Flags? I love that place."

I laughed. "No. It's an expression. You know up and down, emotions and such."

"Ah. I see. Rollercoaster." He raises and lowers his palm. "Good one."

He opens his door and somehow carries me out of the automobile. The shifting and tightening of his muscles beneath my hands and against my side sends delicious shivers across my body. In a whirlwind, I find myself in a large bedroom.

Creams and browns with splashes of turquoise are sprinkled throughout the room. A large bed and even larger windows are all beautifully decorated.

Not the more masculine room I expect from a big hockey star. Has Roman changed his mind?

He throws me on the bed and I bounce.

"The door there," he points, "has extra new toothbrushes and little bottles of shampoo and many things my housekeeper swears people often forget to bring. Go and do whatever girls like to do. I'll bring your bag and leave it outside your door. If you need me, I be in the video room for a little while. You will find it on right to the bottom of stairs."

"Is this your bedroom?"

"No. Across the hall." He stares at me for a moment and my face heats. Not from embarrassment, but from how much I like his staring at me. Then he adds, "You rest. I very much liked kissing you and you did me. So we will talk tomorrow. I want to come to terms so I can kiss your hot pussy and fuck you hard. I want you to suck my big cock. If you want, maybe we make each other happy."

Then he closes the door, and I blink, stunned by his frankness. I need to change my panties. His words have me pulsating.

Present day...

Reminding myself where I'm at now, I shove at the pillows and flip over onto my stomach and pray to go asleep and not dream about Roman. Last thing I need is to get horny at my mom's house. Yuck.

Chapter 4

Roman

I grip my stick harder. If I don't watch myself, I'll be throwing it at Coach Pulkkinen. Not that my stupidity is his fault. I've played in the NHL for seven years and have forgotten a few lessons from my youth. In Russia, you never dump the puck into the corner. We play the puck until we pass or shoot it into the goal.

Tomorrow, I'll do better. Meanwhile, I sit on the bench.

Glancing at the stands, I see the scouts for several NHL teams—two of them are with the Original Six—and twice as many reporters. I had my friend Pavel point them out. He always manages to know. It may seem strange to an outsider why I'm here. I am already an NHL skater but want an NHL scout to notice me. Sometimes to get the proper attention from those in charge, a person has to find a different direction. And a medal will not hurt at all. Maybe then they will stand up and take notice. So here I'm skating in a week-long competition in Russia for I want my employers to see I can be more than an enforcer on the third or fourth line.

When I first went to the States, I thought beating other skaters with my fist was a great way to stand out. Now outstanding stats with record-breaking goals is my objective. I can shine if given the chance.

But my concentration is shit. All I can think of is Kitty.

Kitty, where are you?

I called her three times since arriving. She hasn't answered the house phone. I telephone Casey and he's always jiving about checking on her with no results.

I know she won't cheat on me. She hasn't so far. My fist clenches tight. For all her worldly ways in the bedroom, she's easily fooled by the assholes in the world, including me. I rub my eyes and then squeeze the bridge of my nose. She wouldn't leave without a word to me. Who has tricked her into leaving me? That's the only explanation.

Merely the thought of another man touching her makes my blood boil. The buzzer sounds and the third period is over. Everyone is jumping up and down. I'm happy all went well, but I can't shake my concern about Kitty.

As soon as the clock tells me it's a reasonable time in Atlanta, I'll call her again. If she doesn't answer I will tan her hide—love southern expressions—when I return to the States. No. I'll have to think of something else. She likes spankings too much.

Later, after leaving the showers and brushing off requests to go out and celebrate, I return to the apartment Pavel is renting. I change into gym shorts and a sleeveless tee shirt. I take time to stretch and work out kinks while drinking a couple of jugs of water. Helping the parts of my body recover from being hit or muscles overused is just as important afterwards as it is before.

When I walk into the spare room and slip into bed, it's still too early to call Kitty. So I pound on the hard pillow and sprawl on my back to stare at the ceiling. I rest an arm beneath my head and think back to the first time I spanked her. She came so hard she continued to have sporadic mini climaxes for over five minutes. She hadn't done anything really wrong. That's when I learned she liked to act like a brat to grab my attention.

The week had been a rough one with back-to-back games. We lost both. The team finally had three days before going at it again.

Seven months ago...

Fuck, where did I put my lucky shirt? Rummaging through the laundry room, I don't see it anywhere, not even the dirty clothes hamper. At this rate, I'll be late meeting the newest kid on the team. I promised to teach the rookie a special technique in handling a breaking away. The local practice rink isn't far, but I don't want the kid to think I don't respect him.

"Kitty, where is my favorite t-shirt?" My first Edge t-shirt is so comfortable. No matter how thin it has become, I feel renewed whenever I wear it.

"That old raggedly Edge shirt?"

"Yeah."

"I threw it away."

"What?" I walk into the hallway to see her standing at the other end, chin up and mischief in her eyes.

"You heard me," she says with the cute attitude I'd seen a couple of times since she moved in a month earlier.

I march toward her, and she squeals and runs from me. Seeing her run like a little fairy, on her tiptoes, I know she only taunts me. I catch her around the waist, fling her over my shoulder, and carry her to our bedroom. Her fists pound on my back and hips. They feel like a gentle massage.

"You must be punished for doing that."

"No. I'll be a good girl." She giggles.

I have to fight to keep the grin from my face.

Sitting on the bed, I toss her over my lap and pull her minuscule shorts down her well-rounded butt. I do love the shape and satiny feel of her ass. I run my hands over the tight cheeks and squeeze. She's kicking and shaking her head. I know I won't hurt her. She can easily escape, but confessed not long ago she likes me manhandling her.

I slap her ass, and she shouts at me, "I won't tell you where I hid it."

"So you didn't throw it away."

Her hair flies about her face as she nods vigorously.

Again I smack her butt, watching my handprint appear red on her pale skin.

"Ouch! Why did you do that? I admitted I hadn't thrown it away. It's in my underwear drawer. I wanted to wear it to bed tonight."

With rapid-fire slaps, I turn her ass firetruck red. Her shouts change to groans as her ass lifts to meet my swats. Her breathing becomes loud, matching my own. My dick is so hard it aches. I stop and slide my fingers between her folds. She's creaming like a champ, and I rub her clit until she explodes. Her whole body shakes with her climax.

Unable to hold back any longer, I push her onto her back on the bed, set my shaft free, grab a condom from the nightstand, slip it on with nimble fingers, and slide in deep. I fuck her like a wild man. Her tight pussy squeezes and releases every few seconds. About to shoot my load, I pull out. I want to feel her tighter around my dick.

"No. Please don't stop." She grabs at my shirt. Her pleading fills my ears with sweet music. She plays the game so well. I'm about to explode just from her words.

I pull her hands away. Using her thighs, I flip her onto her stomach, slap her ass for good measure. It's a beautiful sight. All round and red. Then I begin to pound into her slick, pulsating pussy from behind.

She squeals again, but for a different reason. She comes big time as I join her.

The woman is a fun fuck.

Present day...

The memories cause my dick to throb, and I absently rub it. I close my eyes and remember her large tits and how she likes it when I draw hard on those tender tips and then lick and nibble on them. The woman is insatiable. Her desire is as strong as mine. I stroke and thumb my dick's moist head and start jerking my cock.

Her breasts are not the only part I enjoy sucking on. Her sweet little pussy weeps with joy whenever I suck on her clit. I love to run my tongue up and down her slit while I fuck her ass with my fingers. She comes on my face over and over again. She returns the favor by sucking my cock like it's her lifeline.

I yank on my dick until I come with the image of her pink lips stretched around me.

Picking up a shirt from the floor, I use it to clean up. Then head to the shower again. I need something cold on my body before I call her. If I hear her voice at this point, I might come in my pants.

Fifteen minutes later, I have my body under control, and I call my woman. The phone rings and rings and rings. Just before voicemail comes on a man answers.

Hot fury washes over me. What the hell?

Chapter 5

Kitty

The bright morning light shining through the large pane window in the living room bathes my face and body as I head toward the kitchen. Feels so good and revitalizing after the craziness from yesterday. I inhale the heavenly scent of freshly brewed coffee. I want a cup.

Before I step into the kitchen I peek into a mirror near the sofa. First thing I did on waking was apply a little makeup and brush my hair. Mom doesn't allow bedhead at the breakfast table.

When I enter the kitchen, she's watching the news while eating her usual dry wheat toast and scrambled egg. I open a cabinet to get a cup.

"What are you doing?"

I freeze. My fingers barely touch the cup handle. What I'm doing is obvious. So is she asking about my plans today?

"I'm intending to go by the arena. Maybe they'll have a way of contacting Roman for me." Last night, the simple solution had come to me as I drifted off to sleep.

"You don't have a lick of sense. That's not what I asked.

Why are you getting a cup? My coffeemaker makes only two. Enough for me. Go to the convenience store on the corner and get yours. The stuff is expensive enough without you drinking it up." She shakes her head and continues in a lower tone as if I can't hear, "Why was I saddled with a stupid girl? If I had a boy, my life would've been so much easier."

My chest tightens. I take the cup to the sink, and run a little cold water into it. Taking a sip, I keep my back to her while I look out the window at a lonely rose bush. My gaze blurs. Blinking and looking up, I stop the tears. It hurts knowing my mom doesn't love me. I've been told so many times while growing up I'm a burden. Not for the first time I wonder, why hadn't she given me to an adoption agency as a newborn?

The desire for a real family, you know, a mother and father who love their little girl, stings sharper whenever I'm around Mom. I had always wanted a sibling. Someone to tease and to tease me back, to talk about how crazy in love Mom and Dad are and how they embarrassed us with our nude baby pictures, or how they kissed when our friends were over. You know, a TV family. The type of families that don't exist.

I crack open the dishwasher and arrange the cup upside down on the top rack.

"I'll probably be back this evening." I didn't add it all depends on someone believing in what I have to say.

"Chuck and I are going to a party tonight." Chuck Riggins, a former all-star New York Yankee pitcher, retired several decades ago, but he's Mom's go-to companion for society events in Atlanta. He bought her house and pays her utilities. Obviously the woman still has game. Yuck. "I'll not give you a key. Letting you stay for one night is enough. I won't let you mooch off me again. You weren't invited yesterday. You're an adult. Time for you to find your own way. Go and be a nuisance to someone else."

When I was younger, I'd cry and beg her not to say such hateful things. As a teenager, I screamed equally horrible words back at her, solving nothing but making me feel ashamed of myself. So now I ignore her usual venom.

For a few seconds, I stare sightlessly out the window, trying to regain control of my emotions. Taking a deep breath, I turn. I stare over her shoulder at the back door. If I look her in the eyes, she'll know she has the power to hurt me.

"Sure. Goodbye, Mom." A numbness takes over. A feeling I'm so familiar with and have used to protect my wounded heart many times with her.

Did she realize I won't be back? Sleeping in an alleyway or on the streets is preferable. When I need her help or at the very least her sympathy, she turns her back on me. This is the last straw, and this time I mean it. No more expecting her to change and become the mom I had always wished for. That's a waste of good wishes. I pick up my backpack and purse near the door where I left it before coming into the kitchen. Yeah. Deep inside, I continue to hope she will be different, but obviously, my common sense told me to be prepared to leave.

The older woman huffs and continues to stare at the TV.

I wait a second to see if she'll say be careful, or sorry. Only the TV breaks the silence. Taking a deep breath, I open the front door and step outside. A cool breeze plays with my hair. I adjust the strap on my shoulder, and for the last time, I walk down her sidewalk to the street. I ignore the tears flowing down my cheeks.

I've known most of my life that Elaine Summerville cared for no one but herself, but I'm an optimist. That's why I went to my mom's and why I believe Roman has a good excuse for leaving me. There's no guarantee I'll forgive him, but I need to know.

The trip to the arena takes most of the day. Again, I walk the whole way. No point wasting what little money I have on a taxi or bus. As I've been going to the new arena for a few months now, it's no trouble finding the right road on foot without using street signs. With all my determination, I ignore the different men stepping in my path in an effort to draw my attention or shouting catcalls. By the time I arrive at the arena, my nerves are frayed, my feet hurt, and nearly every inch of my body is covered in sweat. Without a cloud in the sky, the sun is brutal.

I wipe off my forehead and the dry tears on my cheeks with an arm and look up.

Above the doors, the mammoth sign shows the four star players for the Edge. Roman told me his face would be up there soon.

I want it for him too.

The ache in my heart intensifies. I feel like I'm chasing a dream. Am I kidding myself? Is my fascination with Roman one-sided? Surely not. He treats me so well. That is until the last month. He's been a little distant and moody, though I did whatever came to mind to cheer him up. As the Edge kept struggling to win games at the end of the season and then the first round of the playoffs, it's no wonder he's acted unlike himself. I know in July his contract with the Edge is coming up. His agent claims he's working on improving the terms. Roman told me how unhappy he'd been with the last one. The agent managed only to get him a little money with only a one-year extension.

For now, I need to find someone who will let me inside the arena and then I can talk with...who? Surely, someone will be there. Management is probably finishing end of season paperwork.

I walk around the building, peeking through glass doors and between the bars of a large gate where they bring in semis hauling equipment for concerts. Whenever the boys are out of town or during the summer months, the arena is used for other events. Finally, I see a man dressed in a security uniform.

"Hey!" I wave when he turns toward me. I recognize him. His name is Sam, and we've spoken to each other several times. He walks up to the gate, a mean look on his face until he gets closer. Then his eyes light up.

"Whatcha doing here? You're number 89's girlfriend, right? Kathy. No. Kitty."

"Yes. Roman Volkov's." Before I can think of how to explain what I need him to do, he looks at what's hanging off my shoulder.

"Where're you going?" he asks, curiosity showing in his dark eyes.

Unsure of how to explain, I start from the beginning. "I need to contact Roman. I woke up yesterday morning and Roman was gone and his agent kicked me out of the house. I don't understand what happened. I need to talk to Roman —"

"Casey Perry's Volkov's agent?"

"Yes. But—"

"No need to explain. The man is a big a-hole. Excuse my language. He's no gentleman. I had a couple run-ins with him. He thinks he's God's gift to the world." The man's kind brown eyes take in my sweaty, grubby appearance.

"Come in and I'll get you a cup of ice water while you tell me the rest. Then we'll see what we can do."

"Thank you, Sam." I walk by his side.

The entrance opens into a cavernous area beneath the arena. A mixture of exhaust and oil assault my nostrils. Along a long cement wall, he opens a small door with a mirror at the top. I walk into a cramped room with a desk and three chairs. Taking a paper cup from a holder nearby, Sam steps into a narrow alcove I didn't notice. When he returns, he hands me the cup. Round chunks of ice float on top of the water. I drink it all. It tastes so good. Even early May in the South can easily hit the eighties.

"Want some more?" He reaches for the cup.

I lean back, holding it away from him, and shake my head. "No, thank you. I'll let the ice melt."

Sam stares at me for a minute, and I begin to squirm. What do I really know about this man? Sure, he's been nice to me many times, but there have been a lot of people around. In fact, why will he help? Kind eyes or not, he knows little about me in return. I might be a crazy ex-girl-friend of Roman's.

With as much subtleness as I can manage, I try to smooth out the wrinkles in my top.

"Tell me the rest of what happened," he prompts.

So I do. Though he looks at me strangely, when I also explain I don't own a cell phone and never had a need before to call Roman, he'd always called me at his home.

"Wait here." He steps out of the tiny office.

Through the glass I see him. It's a two-way mirror. He's talking on his cell phone. He shakes his head as if the person he's talking to can see him. At least a minute crawls by and then he turns back to the door as he slips the phone into his pocket.

I step away to pretend to look at an Edge calendar on the wall, thumbing through the months. Turns out Roman is Mr. July. He's wearing his shoulder pads and chest protector without a shirt. He looks like a sexy, badass warrior.

"Come with me. We're going to talk with my boss." He holds his hand out for me to pass him and points to the steel door.

If he plans to kick me out, we wouldn't be heading toward an elevator.

Before we entered the elevator, Sam stops me.

"Do you have a Facebook or Instagram account with more than one picture of you and Mr. Volkov together at his home?"

Players pose for pictures all the time, but usually only with close friends at their homes.

"Roman told me the Facebook one belongs to some fan. He prefers Instagram, but they're only of his games and he forgets to keep it up to date." He's been burned by the social media sites a couple of times. The man has a problem keeping his mouth shut about certain teams he plays against. "I don't have a computer or phone, so I've never bothered with the sites."

"You're certainly different from any woman of your age I've ever met. Though I have to say it sounds smart." He shakes his head and smiles. His deep chuckle helps me to relax.

"How about I take a picture of you?" He must have seen the concern on my face. "It will help to confirm your story, okay? That's why I asked about your media accounts."

"Sure." Should I have said no? I mentally shrug. For what good reason? A lot of players have live-in girlfriends. I have nothing to hide. No warrants. No lies. I don't even owe money.

We enter the elevator. How will his boss treat me? People can be so judgmental at times. On the surface, he could see a woman living and mooching off a man. He wouldn't know the real me or that I'm living the only life I know.

After a slow, nerve-racking elevator ride, we walk down an empty hallway with framed action shots of the team. I can hear people talking as I follow Sam. Glancing into the open doorways, I notice some rooms have one person and others a half dozen. On reaching a closed door with the words Public Safety engraved on a brass rectangle, Sam opens it and motions for me to proceed him.

A lean man with a military haircut rises to his feet. He smiles, but it doesn't reach his eyes. Am I stupid for coming here? Where will I go if they escort me out and off the property? I have only a few dollars and nowhere else to go since Mom doesn't want me to bother her again.

"This is Robert Wall. He's my boss. He'll help. Tell him what happened," Sam says in a soft voice behind me before he closes the door. Tired and feeling a little scared, I'm sure he's about to read me the riot act by saying I'm a trouble-maker, and I better not darken their door ever again.

"So you claim to be Volkov's girl?"

"Yes, sir. We've been living together since early October." I wipe my sweating hands on my jeans. The man speaks in an even tone, but his cold stare scares the crap out of me. I feel as if I've done something wrong, but I know I haven't.

"At his condo?" he asks.

"House. He's never mentioned owning a condo." I

understand he's testing me. I wonder how many girls have claimed a nonexistent relationship with one of the skaters?

"I sent your photo to the coach's wife. Will she claim she knows you? Might as well confess now. She's met every skater's significant other."

Oh, no. He's going to bother Millie. Will she remember me? I'm not that memorable. If she does, she'll think I'm a troublemaker bringing her into my troubles. She will tell the coach. He might remember me sticking my tongue at Roman's agent.

"Ms. Summerville, do you need more time to think of a good lie?" Mr. Wall asks, bringing me back to the here and now.

My face heats. I take pride in telling the truth and rarely losing my temper. Living with my volatile mother taught me to control it. Shouting and name-calling never serves a purpose, but the man's attitude is pushing me to the edge. I'm so weary and want to go home. Only I don't have one.

"I'm sorry but after walking here from my mom's house, I'm tired and my brain is a little slow." His expression tells me he believes I'm stalling.

"Where does your mom live?"

I tell him.

His eyebrows lift. "That's a long ways to walk."

"I doubt the coach's wife will remember me though it was only a couple nights ago when we met for the first time at the charity costume party. At games, I don't sit with the other wives and girlfriends. I like sitting near the glass so Roman and I can see each other."

In the family suite, the women always look like models even in baggy jerseys with their hair, face, and nails done to perfection. They are so far out of my league. I'm just a puck bunny and nothing more. And whenever Roman tries to talk me into flying out with a few of the women on a road trip or two, I make an excuse. I'm afraid to be alone in airports and planes. It's a pain to be a wimp. So I know mainly his teammates from visits to his house and the few parties we've attended together.

"Excuse me."

I look up. A tall, red-headed man stood in the doorway, his hands on his hips. His forehead wrinkles with concern. Relief flows through my body. Ryan is Roman's best friend on the team. He was with him when we met the first time.

"What can I help you with, Mr. Schmid?" Mr. Wall's frustration is clear as he tries to rein in his glare.

"I was signing pucks in the back of the team store and overheard Kitty was here." He steps inside the office.

"Hey, Ryan." I try to smile but fail miserably from Ryan's worried expression.

The security manager clears his throat.

Ryan starts first. "Robert, what has Kitty done?"

"You know her?"

"Yeah. She's Roman's girlfriend. They've been together several months now." He shoots a smile my way. "I think he's a dumb-ass for leaving her behind."

Before I know it, I'm strolling down another hallway, but this time with Ryan. He stops and waves me through a doorway. I enter a beautiful conference room that looks over the Atlanta skyline.

"Don't worry. We'll figure this all out. When I get ahold of Roman, I'll burn his ass for leaving you alone. I don't understand why he didn't ask me to look after you." Ryan pats my shoulder. I can tell he wants to comfort me, but is unsure of how to go about it without stepping over the line with his best friend's girl.

My throat clogs and eyes burn. It feels funny to have

someone besides Roman to worry about me. Yet, from everything I know to this point, Roman isn't worried. For some reason, he just plain forgot I exist.

I blink away the moisture in my eyes. This isn't the time or place for a pity party. Once today is enough. Actually, I rarely cry. Mom told me when I was younger I wasn't normal. She doesn't know me. I'm human and can only withstand being rejected or forgotten so many times before I fall apart. But I've learned my tears never made my situation better as a kid, so why would it help being older? I carefully wipe beneath my eyes, making sure not to smear my eyeliner or mascara. I see enough pity in his and the guard's eyes. No need to look pitiful too.

"Hello," a deep voice interrupts the silence.

A tall, handsome, middle-age man enters the room. Mr. McMillan. With his deep-brown almost-black hair, equally dark eyes, and handsome face marred by a scar bisecting one bold eyebrow, the ferocious scowl can cause anyone to tremble. Though I'm nervous around him, I feel deep inside that he's a kind man. Maybe it was something Roman said which I don't remember that set up the feeling. Or the way he and his wife teased each other about the dog.

I force my feet to stay put, ignoring the urge to run as I remind myself, like several times already this morning, I have nowhere to go.

Unsure my voice will work, I nod, giving an unsteady smile.

"Hey, Coach. You know Kitty, Roman's girl?" Ryan waves his hand my way.

"Yeah, we met at the Paws and Claws charity." His dark gaze turns to me. "Hello there, Kitty." He reaches out to shake my hand. It feels odd to clasp it. What can I say, people I meet scarcely offer their hand. "Robert and Sam filled me in on what happened. So Roman left and decided to have his agent throw you out?"

My chest clenches for, like, the hundredth time today. Embarrassment heats my cheeks. The man gets to the point.

"Yes."

"His agent is Casey Perry," he says more as a confirmation than a question.

"Yes." My voice is barely above a whisper. He has a murderous expression on his face. I'm not sure if the look is aimed at me or the agent.

"I have no idea what the bastard is up to while Roman is gone," Ryan says. "I've never cared for Perry. No way would Roman have him do his dirty work."

Mr. McMillan crosses his arms over his chest.

I did notice Ryan never said anything about Roman wanting me to stay or had feelings for me. Once again, am I hoping for validation for staying with the man?

"He likes to manipulate people," Mr. McMillan adds his thoughts on Perry. "Agents should be good at it, but to shoot straight at the heart of the situation. I've never seen him work any deals to his client's advantage." On seeing my confused look, he rubs his scarred eyebrow. He appears uncomfortable with his own candid opinion. "Returning to the problem at hand, let's see if we can get you situated until Roman returns. Ramsey Fournier, he's the general manager, probably knows a way of contacting Roman. So we should know what the hell is going on tonight or no later than tomorrow morning."

My shoulders feel a little lighter. He sounds certain. I smile. "Thank you."

"No problem. For now, come with me. I called Millie, and she said she'll kick my ass if I don't bring you home and let her feed you. We agreed that you need to stay until we get this straightened out."

I blink. "Excuse me?"

"You remember meeting my wife the other night?" His voice softens and one corner of his mouth lifts.

"Yes." I smile back. For a stern-looking man, he has a soft side.

"Then come on." He waits for me to walk ahead of him out of the conference room.

It appears I will be spending the night with Mr. McMillan's family. This will be unique. I've never stayed with a regular family before, one with a mom and dad.

This will be interesting.

Chapter 6

Roman

"Who the hell are you?" I growl.

"Roman, it's me. Casey."

I finally recognize my agent's voice.

"Put Kitty on the fucking phone." I grit my teeth. I want to tear the man's heart by way the throat for not rushing over and doing what I asked days ago. Kitty is probably in a panic. Note or not, I promised to call after I settled in. Why hadn't she waited by the phone? She usually does whatever I tell her. Not that she's a pushover, but I can tell she likes to make me happy and, fuck, she makes me happy.

"She's not here, man. I don't know where she is. I looked in every room. She didn't leave a note. It looks like most of her shit is gone too."

"What the fuck are you talking about?"

"No makeup in any of the bathrooms. I did see a few of her outfits hanging in a closet in your bedroom. Nothing in the drawers. Maybe she'll be back for more. Hell, she could've wiped out your safe, I wouldn't know."

"I told you in my email to go the morning I left." The man is irritating the hell out of me. He'd assured me at the party he would look after her if I received good news. The man owes me.

"I did but I left the key at the office you gave me. No one answered the door. I thought she might still be in bed, but she must've left then." The sympathy in the man's voice didn't make me feel any better.

"You better find her. I need to concentrate here. I need to know she's okay." Pleading mixed with anger came out of my mouth.

"Damn, you need to write her off. She's dragging you down by playing her mind games. I'll probably find her fucking one of your buddies. Once a puck bunny, always a fuck bunny."

"You're full of shit. Just do what I say!" I end the call and throw my phone onto the bed. I need my rest, but worrying about Kitty and what she's doing is driving me mad.

With a flick of my wrist, I shove back the covers and pull out a square of silk. A little bit of heat dots my face. It's something when a bruiser like me blushes over sneaking a girl's pillow case out of the laundry and slip it into his suit-case to sleep with. The material still has her scent. A mixture of hot beaches and summer rain. My cock begins to swell. Fuck, the last thing I need is a hard-on. I won't get any sleep. And if I give in to my right hand and shoot my load, I will still be restless. That has been proven. It's been months since I've given into self-abuse and here I will be doing it a second time since leaving home. Kitty gives the best head and cheerfully greets me on her knees when I return from a long road trip. The girl is special.

The thought of her puffy lips surrounding my cock and sucking hard causes me to groan. The woman is an artist when it comes to blow jobs.

I start down the hall to the bathroom to take another quick cold shower. I need a break. I need sleep. I need to keep my mind on the game tomorrow.

I'm feeling high as I skate along the bench and bump gloves. My body's humming. A few seconds ago, I dropped in my first hat trick since I played with the Atlanta Edge affiliate, Louisville Lions. Those were the days. I always managed two to three a season back then.

"You're on fire, Volkov," one of my teammates shouts.

I nod and fight the full-blown grin wanting to surface. Just not cool to show too much happiness. Can't have the other team believing I'm rubbing it in. Unsportsmanlike behavior and all.

Sore fucking losers.

We wait for the ref to drop the puck during face-off. The clock has ten seconds left. My teammates and I know we have this game in our pockets as we're three ahead.

You're welcome.

We play keep away and before I know it, we're raising our sticks and then bumping fists and rubbing helmets. When I finally reach the locker room, I take a shower and dress. Years of practice at leaving the outside world behind while I concentrate on the game helps me place my concern about Kitty in a corner of my brain. Now it's at the forefront and I want to find a private place to call my house again, and if no answer, then my agent.

"Come, Roman. We need to celebrate. Before you know it, we'll be enjoying the summer as champions." Pavel slaps my back and follows the crowd out of the players exit. I look at the big clock on the wall and subtract the hours. It's afternoon in Atlanta. A good time to call.

"Yes. Go on. I need to make a call." I wave him on. Pavel looks at me with sympathy. I don't want anyone's pity. "Fine, fine. I'll come now and call her afterwards. It won't be too late."

He laughs and bows, rolling a hand in a flourish. "Oh, master of the hat trick, let me help you find a good Russian puck bunny to make you forget your runaway American. Russian vodka and Russian women. Perfect medicine for what ails you."

As soon as I walk into the bar, I realize I don't want anything to do with the women. After I finish my drink and shout the usual inane obscenities and goodbyes to my team-mates, I order a cab.

Within moments of reaching Pavel's place, I punch in my number. Ringing continues until my voicemail comes on. I can't leave her a voicemail. She probably doesn't even know how to retrieve it. She never received calls. It always bothered me she didn't, but she always said her friends are too busy. That bothered me too.

Next, I call my agent's number. No answer. I have a feeling the bastard is ignoring me. Then an idea comes to me, and I try a new number. Why in the hell I hadn't thought of it before frustrates me.

"Hey, Ryan, I need a favor."

He laughs. "Hello there, you crazy Russian. Do you ever check your voicemail?"

I like the good-natured, big guy. A good laid-back drinking buddy and a hockey-sense center.

"No." Actually, I have looked but only looked for those from home or my agent. "First, why I call, I can't find my girl. You know, Kitty. Could you go by my house and see if she's been there recently and ask the other guys if they've seen her?"

I wait for Ryan to tell me one of my teammates has sweet-talked her into staying with him. She's such a soft-hearted woman. I'll break every finger of the man who touches her.

"What are you talking about, man? Have you been smoking crack? You should've listened to my message. Why did you leave her without a word?" His tone ends on a reproachful tone.

"What the hell are *you* talking about?" I return the same question.

"It's simple. She showed up at the arena yesterday asking for help."

"Help? Is she okay?" None of this is making sense. I'm too far away to be there for her.

"She's fine, but upset." I relax when Ryan says that. "She's confused with your disappearance. Scared even."

"I don't understand. She knows." I have no idea what game she's playing, but I need to talk with her. "Where is she now? Tell her to come to the phone."

"She's with Coach."

"Coach? Why?"

"He believed her story about you leaving without saying a word."

"What the fuck?" This is beyond belief. "You know me better than that." Then I told Ryan my side of the story.

"I see," he says. "You really should've talked to her instead. I don't know what happened to the note. Your agent is a real tool. Maybe he got to it first and destroyed it."

"No way." I say that while remembering the caustic words Casey said over the months since Kitty moved in and even more recently. It is something to think about.

"Don't be a stubborn ass. Kitty told us what happened after you disappeared on her. I believe her. That asshole threatened to kick her out the day you left if she didn't . . . uh, didn't put out for him."

By the time I hang up, I'm pulling at my hair. What is going on? Whatever it is, I'll get it straightened out. I punch in the numbers Ryan gave me. There had never been a need to call my head coach. My agent talked with him or the G.M. Most of the day-to-day information for the forwards is handled through the assistant coach.

The number rings and rings and finally voicemail comes on. "McMillan. Leave a message." The man does not waste words.

"Hey, Coach, Volkov here. I heard Kitty with you. Ask her to call me on number showing up on your phone." I hesitate for a moment. "Be sure she calls me." As soon as I hang up, I regret not saying more.

Hell, I don't know what it would've been. Possibly like telling her I'm sorry? Fuck. I don't remember ever telling a woman I'm sorry. My papa believes saying sorry is pointless without actions backing it up. Ryan said she's scared and confused. I hate to think of my kitten being scared.

What the hell can I do to make it up to Kitty while over five thousand miles away?

Chapter 7

Kitty

The ride from the arena to Mr. McMillan's house takes forever. He concentrates on driving and says little. He only tells me to be sure to wear my seatbelt, and then asks if I'm comfortable with the temperature. When we pull into a long, landscaped road, I quickly realize it's his driveway. The freaking man has a mansion. I don't know what I expected, but wow. Roman's house is the size of a quaint cottage in comparison.

The McMillan house is actually a log cabin times ten. Huge, carved double doors part to reveal a spacious room with a mix of modern and traditional decor. I struggle to keep my jaw from dropping. The open concept living, dining room areas can easily hold my mom's whole house. I relish how the A-frame with tall glass windows lets in the sunlight without being harsh. All of the furniture is deep and comfortable looking. Perfect for the broad-shouldered man leading the way into the interior of the house.

"Millie, we're home," he shouts as soon as we walk in.

I continue to follow Mr. McMillan past a long dining table and into a massive kitchen that overlooks the backyard's lazy river and pool. As a kid I dreamed of having one, but nothing like the huge layout of the McMillan's. It's amazing. I itch to try it out. That's unlikely as I'm only staying one night. Anyway, I don't have a swimsuit.

With a sigh, I turn my back on the gorgeous view and meet the kind, hazel eyes of Millie McMillan.

"So nice to see you again. Kitty, right?"

"Yes, ma'am." One thing about living and growing up in the South, I know how to show respect to my hostess. Saying "yes, ma'am" and "no, ma'am" are ingrained into my DNA. "Thank you, Mrs. McMillan, for letting me stay today. I'll find a place tomorrow." I didn't exactly lie. I will find a safe alley to sleep in. Telling them that will make me sound pitiful. They feel sorry enough for me. No way can I admit I have nowhere to go.

"Please call me Millie. I enjoyed meeting you at the party and wished I had gotten to talk with you some more. Now I'll get a chance. You know, the other night I felt like we'd met before. You look so familiar. Had we met before then?"

"No, ma'am." I didn't know what else to say.

The magnificent place and the kindness shown by the rich and famous couple have rattled my brains. Making small talk with strangers hasn't been a strong suit of mine, not until Roman. Somehow I feel relaxed with her.

"That's okay. You probably remind me of someone. I'm sure it will come to mind." She turns and waves us over to a high table with four tall chairs. Perfect for a cozy meal. "I made Guy's favorite cabbage borscht. It's more of a winter meal, but really good anytime. I have cornbread to go with it. When living in the South..." She laughs and shrugs, and starts pulling out glasses to fill them with ice. "What flavor of pop do you want?"

"Water will be fine for me." I look around, trying to find the bathroom.

"If you want to wash your hands, there's a guest toilet down that hall." Mr. McMillan points to a small hallway.

"Thank you." I hurry toward the direction he indicates.

The little room is simply decorated in blues and grays. Without wasting time—I didn't want them to think I'm being nosey and snooping in other rooms—I clean up and walk into the kitchen, surprising the couple kissing.

"Sorry." I turn away.

Millie laughs. The woman is so cheerful. I'm a little jealous. Not of her relationship with Mr. McMillan. Uh, no. It's because I wish Roman and I had their type of relationship. What does a girl like me know about normal?

Anyone meeting my mom would understand. Not having a steady male role model around, I think of and treat men differently from what I've seen on TV. When I was a child, I thought men were almost god-like: they controlled where my caregivers lived, they were strong and their temper something to fear, and the women I knew placed them on a pedestal.

Of course, as I grew older, I knew they were not perfect, feet of clay and all that.

"No, no. Come in. Have a seat here." I climb up on the seat beside Millie with Mr. McMillan on the far side of his wife. The chairs are made for tall people and I hook my ankles to keep from falling off.

The borscht is different from the kind Roman taught me how to make. This one has a sweet tang, but I like it. I'm so hungry. It's been a long day.

"Delicious." I'm glad I said it out loud. Millie's face lights up.

"Guy's mom gave me the recipe. Though mine is still

missing something, Edna's is superb, mine isn't worth shaking a stick at." She smiles at her husband and dips in her spoon for another bite.

"Don't let her fool you. It's as good as Mom's. Even Dad agrees." Mr. McMillan sips from his soda and winks at me.

It confuses me. Is he coming on to me? Or is the wink only a joking gesture with the conversation? I desperately want to believe the latter. I like Millie so much and don't want to believe her husband is a lecher. Surely not. He never said a wayward word or made a suspicious gesture toward me in the car. The usual vibes are not there.

Yes. It's merely a friendly gesture. I'm not used to having men around who aren't looking at me as a possible conquest. One of the drawbacks in growing up without a dad, with the few men around always on the prowl, even my mom's boyfriends.

"Yeppers. But he also said not to tell your mother he admitted it," she reminds him.

This time I laugh too. They make it so easy to relax.

The conversation continues and they ask me a few questions about my parents. I just say my father isn't in the picture and my mom lives on her own.

They don't want the sad details.

Yes. I like this couple. I wish I had a mom and dad like them. Their kids are so lucky. I'm only three years older than their son in college. He plays hockey and has already signed up with another team once he finishes Harvard. From what I take from their conversation, he's a genius in the classroom and on the ice.

Presently, the two younger kids still live at home and are in school today. Though the middle child, a boy of sixteen, is moving to Illinois after this summer to stay with the family's friends and play on a junior league.

The daughter, the baby of the family, is dealing them fits with her growing interest in a quarterback at the local high school. From the way they talk, I'm not sure if they are upset because their daughter is interested in a boy or that the boy doesn't play hockey.

"Enough about us and our kids. How did you and Roman meet?" Millie lifts her empty bowl and picks up her husband's. I follow her to the sink with my own.

"My boyfriend had broken up with me at a restaurant." She doesn't need to know the whole sordid story, including that it happened in Nashville and not here. "I was sitting in the booth trying to decide what I should do when Roman slipped in next to me and started flirting. He was so sweet. What about you and Mr. McMillan?"

Millie hooks her arm through her husband's. "Guy was drinking with friends, and they laid bets he couldn't talk me into going home with him. He told them not only would he take me home, I would be screaming his name before the night was over."

I blink. I can't believe they are telling me, a stranger, this story.

"Honey, you shocked our young friend here," he says in a teasing tone.

A lightness comes to my shoulders, heck, my whole body. He called me a friend. I know he doesn't mean it, but I appreciate his kindness. He's still talking. I turn my attention back to the conversation.

"Hurry and tell the rest of the story." Mr. McMillan kisses her on the cheek and moves to the table, picking up the glasses and sitting them in the sink. I watch in amazement as he wipes the countertop. I've never seen a man pick up and clean—maybe his fancy new car—but never in a kitchen. Roman wouldn't know where his dishwasher sat unless it exploded.

"You don't have to." I raise my hands. Did I want to know the details?

"Oh, it's not what you think." Millie laughs into her hand. "He decided to turn the tables on his friends. I drove him home because he acted drunk."

"I had only one beer, but I needed you at my house and that was the fastest way to convince you."

"I had a friend to follow in his car."

"Yep. She didn't trust me yet."

"But I still helped you inside. You could've been a serial killer, but your dimples suckered me in. I stayed and sent my friend home in my car." Millie gazes at Mr. McMillan with such good humor, I'm a puddle of envy.

"I'm a bit of a sweet-talker too."

"More like fast-talker." Millie is laughing so hard now, she's having to hold onto the counter to stand. Her husband shakes his head but the love shining from his eyes almost takes my breath away.

"Well, I had to or you would've left and I needed your help in teaching my friends a lesson." He chuckles.

Wiping her eyes, Millie regains her composure. "Sorry, but considering what a horndog Guy was in the day, it takes everything in me to keep a straight face when I think about what we did."

"How did he win his bet, if you don't mind me asking?" As hard as they are laughing, I'm guessing it's a good story. I have a feeling, at the time, they hadn't made wild monkey sex all night.

"Let's say he had no problem collecting his bet. Wait, wait, it's not what you think. See, he was roommates with two of his friends. So when they came in early that morning, hung over and desperate for sleep, we started jumping up and down on Guy's squeaky bed, screaming each other's names for about fifteen minutes. They banged on the bedroom door, begging us to quit, declaring Guy the winner." Millie's arms circle her husband's waist as she smiles up at him. "We've been together ever since."

"You're shameless," he whispers.

Though I'm a couple feet away, I can still hear.

"The way you like it."

"Yep." He looks up and sees me staring. Something crosses his face as if he's disturbed by my fascination and quickly his expression becomes blank. "Let me go out to the car and get your stuff.

I had totally forgotten my backpack.

"Thank you so much." I feel like I'm in another dimension. I really thought these sort of people only live on television. You know. Like, not for real.

Millie turns to me. "Kitty is a nickname, right? I used to know a sister and brother named Sundance and Butch. The parents were big fans of the movie." A bewildered look washes over her. "I only hoped they weren't fans of the real-life criminals." Then she laughs. "I just thought of that. Goodness, I hope not."

"It's short for Kathleen."

"What a beautiful name. I'm a little biased when it comes to old names. Mine is Millicent. And my kids have old-fashioned names. Is it okay for me to call you Kathleen or Kathy?"

I wrinkle my nose. "Mom named me after her mother. Mom did that hoping Grandma Kathleen would accept her out of wedlock kid. She never did." The compassion in Millie's eyes bothers me. Why did I tell her that? I have a big mouth around her. She's so easy to talk to, but I don't want anyone pitying me. I got over the rejection a long time ago. Besides, the stern old woman has been dead since I was ten. "You can call me Katie." One of Mom's old boyfriends called me that. He was nice. I had hoped he would become my dad. Like all the rest, he left one day and never came back.

"Katie. I like that." She pats my hand.

I like her. She and Mr. McMillan make a great couple. So light-hearted and in love, and willing to take in a stranger.

"Thank you for letting me stay the night. I'll have some-place to stay by tomorrow."

"Don't worry about that. You'll stay until Roman returns, and we'll get this straightened out," Mr. McMillan says, as he walks back into the kitchen carrying my back-pack. "Follow me and we'll get you settled in."

I hang back a few steps as he heads down a long hall and then up a flight of stairs. I hear Millie's footsteps behind me.

"You can stay in Sam's old room." She waves a hand toward the bed. Her husband drops my backpack at the foot.

The room is painted a light blue with white trim. A few hockey posters cover one wall and shelves of trophies are lined up on the opposite one. An opened door leads into a bathroom. Wow. He had his own private bathroom. How would it feel to be a kid with such luxury? The bed is large with a dark red-and-blue comforter. Everything is neat and orderly. I'm afraid to touch anything.

"If you don't think he'll mind." I remember Mr. McMillan saying their oldest son, Samuel, is in his junior year at Harvard.

"No. Sam isn't due back home until next June and only

for a short stay. Since his dad's tied up with the team, there isn't much time between one season and another."

I almost ask, what about her? Then catch myself. No need to make her feel bad about her son not making time to see her.

"Micah's at training camp and should be back in a couple days, and Hannah is spending the night with a friend."

My face becomes hot. "I'm so sorry. You probably were planning a date night without kids, and I ruined it."

"No. You didn't. I have an early meeting in the morning." Mr. McMillan rests an arm over his wife's shoulder.

"Okay. Thank you again for letting me stay." I don't know what else to say. I hope my voice conveys my heartfelt feelings.

"No problem. Relax. If you need anything just let me know." Millie pats my arm.

"Night." Mr. McMillan nods and walks out with his wife.

I gingerly sit on the edge of the bed. I feel like I'm in a dream. One where parents care about their children and treat strangers with kindness. Wide-eyed, I look around and tears begin to fall. I swipe at them. Boy, cry one time and I'm Niagara Falls. Looking around, I'm all alone. Am I destined not to have a life like this with Roman? How can I? I have no idea how to go about it.

Chapter 8

Roman

What the fuck?

I stare at the scoreboard, watching the clock count down to less than five minutes in the third period. But that's not what's bothering me. Hell, we're leading by two points. Unless we really fuck up, we have this game.

My anger started twenty-four hours ago, and will be twenty-six hours or more when I return back to the apartment and check my voicemail. No cell phones allowed in the locker room. What can I say? The current team's coach wants our full attention whenever we're at the arena. One full day has gone by since I left a message with Coach McMillan for Kitty to call me back. Not one word so far from either of them. Could Ryan be wrong? Maybe she's not staying with Coach's family?

A loud bang jerks me out of my thoughts. In front of the bench, one of our defensemen exchanges curses with the opposing team's center after slamming him into the boards and almost tipping the opponent onto the players' laps. We all lean back, not wanting to get hit with a flying stick. A

71

teammate chirps about the skater almost giving us a lap dance, and we all laugh.

Damn. I have to be careful and stay aware of my surroundings. Never have I let a woman take my mind off a game until now. I'm so fucking worried about her. Two more games, four more days, and it's over and I can go back to the States. I've never wished for time during a game to go by so fast. Once it is over, I'll know if the rest of my career will be set. I want Kitty to be proud of me.

Where did that come from? When did I care about what any woman thought of me? I usually keep my attention on the prize, being on the top line to prove I can be the skater they want there.

I stand and prepare to climb over the board. Time for my line to take the ice. No more thinking of anything but the game.

An hour later, I'm in the showers. The third period went well. I'd managed to keep my mind on the business of scoring and blocking, ending the game with a goal and three assists. I'm feeling good, but the nagging worry about Kitty is pulling me down.

"Hey, hurry up, Volkov. We need to celebrate. There's a high-class gentleman's club promising us free drinks if we show up." Pavel dries off. "I don't want to hear anything about your American girlfriend. You act like an old married man."

Maybe that's what I need. A night of stress-free thoughts. No staring at the walls, waiting for a call that isn't coming anytime soon.

"I'm in. Give me a few minutes."

When I walk out into the humid night air, the persistent unease settles in the back of my mind.

I hope I won't regret tonight.

Maybe Pavel is right. I act like an old married man. Besides, what can go wrong? Many times I've partied with teammates, and we all became closer. A solid team. The most that has gone wrong is some broken glasses. We pay the manager and nothing more happens.

Hell, I deserve a night of carefree fun. I know how to handle myself. I'm single and over the age of consent.

No regrets to be concerned about.

The back of my neck itches with nagging anxiety.

I shake it off and jog to the waiting car.

Chapter 9

Kitty

I toss and turn in the borrowed bed. I want Roman's warmth resting against mine. By midnight, I sink into the mattress and dream about what happened a few weeks back. It's so vivid. I'm certain I can reach out and touch him.

One month ago...

"Hey, Kitty, get your ass in here."

"I'm coming." I slam a drawer closed as I lift the tube of lotion he likes rubbed into his bruises. Down the length of one side he's black and blue with hints of red at the edges. I had seen the hit during the game and knew he'd need my attention after the athletic trainer tended to his bruise. If I didn't know how much he loved playing, I would beg him to quit. Not that he will do it for me, but maybe he'd think about it.

My heart picks up speed. As always, the sight of the big man, naked and stretched face down across the huge bed, fires up my blood. There is nothing like having a well-toned, strong man's body between my legs and beneath my ass as I straddle his hips. I squeeze the cream onto my palm and let it warm before I gently spread it over his ribs and then carefully rub it in. One of the trainers had given me tips on how to do it without hurting him more.

The long moan he gives tells me I did it right. When I finish, I rest on top of him, my bare breasts press to his muscled back. There is nothing better than his hot, taut male skin against mine. Well, almost. I slide my hand underneath him, above his hipbone, and reach his hard cock. Men have the most interesting equipment, and I'm fortunate to be holding a prime example.

"Damn. Your grip is perfect. Strong and certain." He grunts.

I like the sounds he makes when I do something he enjoys. I thumb the moist slit and another grunt comes out loud and turns into a moan. I giggle.

"What's so funny?" His husky voice almost sounds angry, but I know he's only turned on. The room twirls and I'm on my back and he's on all fours above me. His hair falls across his eyes.

"You sound like a wild animal." I move the strands to the side and caress the scar across his brow.

"Animal, huh?" He smiles and then pretends to be serious, growling and snapping his teeth. "Maybe I'll eat you up." He nips at my shoulder.

Crazily, my body trembles with need as my clit throbs.

He leans down and licks and then gently tugs at one nipple with his teeth. I arch into his mouth and sigh. He moves to the other one, sucking in the hard tip and bites me. I shriek. Before I recover, he drags his tongue down the center of my torso. The wet end dips into my belly button and trails lower. And in seconds, he laps between my legs, toying with the tender flesh. I open my mouth and silently exhale as I orgasm.

Present day...

Why silently? Odd as I'm never quiet when I come.

Consciousness dissipates the dream. Oh, yes, I'm in his coach's house.

But all alone.

I force my eyes open. It is only a memory revisited in my sleep, but one of the many sexy times I miss so much.

Pain rips through me with his betrayal. Knowing hockey is his number one love does not make him leaving without a word any easier. I can't see anything but the clock on the nightstand. The soft, yellow numbers on the clock declare it to be three in the morning.

Where is he at this moment? Is he with another woman? My insides shred by the soul-wrenching thought. From the chitchat I overheard from his friends, he never missed out on female companionship before he met me. He hasn't made me any promises. I have to move on and quit thinking and dreaming about him.

Tears well up and trickle down my cheeks. I stuff one corner of the Edge blanket I brought from his house into my mouth. Then I cover my face with the pillow to keep quiet. I don't want to upset them with my sadness. How pitiful will that be? I clench my teeth. This stupid crying must stop. All of the emotions swirling in my brain and heart are exhausting. Slowly my muscles let go and I drift into total darkness.

What feels like seconds later, I wake up to sunshine. Someone is knocking on the bedroom door. Struggling to sit up, I wipe the sleep from my eyes. Without a mirror I know I look like crap. I watch the doorknob turn.

"Katie, are you awake?" I don't recognize the voice.

Then the door opens. In walks a tall, almost anorexic-thin teenaged girl. Her blonde hair and pretty hazel eyes certainly give her away. The only daughter.

"Yes. I'm awake. You must be Hannah." I smile, hoping I don't scare her off. I finger comb my hair, making sure it's not standing straight up.

"Hi. Mom wanted me to let you know she has breakfast ready." Her curiosity is as obvious as my own. How is it to grow up with such kind parents?

I sniff the air. The scent of bacon and coffee drift in. My stomach reminds me how little I ate yesterday.

"I'll be down as soon as I get dressed. Thank you." When she continues to stand there, I raise my eyebrows in silent question.

"Roman," she says hesitatingly, "is he, you know, as awesome to be around as he appears?" Her face reddens.

Ah, a fan.

"Actually, yes." I always thought so before two days ago. No need to drag out my dirty laundry in front of the whole family, if her mom and dad haven't.

"I just knew he was. He says hi to me when the team comes to my parents' parties. So many of them are afraid of Dad and won't even look at me, but he makes me feel like I'm not invisible."

As pretty as she is I'm sure they look, but between her youth and her dad, they work hard to act like they don't. Roman is fearless when it comes to flirting with females, old or young. To a young teenager, his charisma has to be nearly overwhelming.

"He's a nice guy." And I mean what I say. That's why I'm having such a hard time believing he kicked me out of his house without an explanation.

Of course, I couldn't imagine it happening to me the

other times when I lived with a Vezna Trophy winner and then almost three years later to a James Norris winner. I do enjoy hockey and the men who are physically fit from playing the sport. Mom said I got the hang-up from her. How could I not? She watches nearly every game on TV. I suspected one of the teams had my dad on it. She never said who. Mom said hockey was all he thought of and he was a selfish asshole. Obviously, the attraction to the same type of men runs in the family.

"I play hockey for the Atlanta Lady Birds." Hannah pulls me back. She twists her lips as if waiting for me to say something negative about a girl playing hockey.

"That's great. I would love to see you play. What position?"

Her eyes twinkle. I know I said the right thing.

"Netminder."

With her height, I bet her coach gave her no option.

"Do you like it?"

"Yeah. But it's scary sometimes. If I don't keep my concentration on the puck, I can easily lose the game. Then the team's mad at me."

"Then shame on your teammates. They should know their goalie has to be protected. If they don't, you'll get bombarded. More shots on the net, more of a chance the opposing team gets a goal. You can't do it all on your own."

Her face breaks into a big grin. "It's so nice to talk to someone new who not only understands hockey but is female too. I get tired of explaining the game to people in the South."

"More are learning." I stand and stretch. Though I'm wearing an oversized T-shirt, I quickly put my hands down when I realize it's riding up too high.

I hear Millie hollering from the kitchen, "Hannah, come on and bring Katie with you."

"Oh, I got sidetracked." She nods toward the hallway. "I'll tell her you're changing and will be down soon."

"Thanks."

She walks to the door and, as she's about to close it, turns. "You're as sweet as Mom said." Then she disappears into the hallway.

I close the door and rest my back against it. She told her daughter I'm sweet. The feeling is mutual. Every family member I've met so far have been exceptionally nice to me.

My stomach growls. I rush to clean up and change into a pair of shorts and an old T-shirt Roman gave me.

When I trot downstairs to eat, I cautiously look around. Millie gives me an odd look.

"Is it just us girls?" I ask.

"Guy has a meeting downtown and will be gone for the day," Millie says as she nods to the table and then smiles. The woman smiles a lot, but not the fake kind, for her eyes match her expression.

My stiff shoulders relax. "Sorry for being so obvious. I think he disapproves of me."

"Don't be silly. He's concerned by the way Roman has treated you." Millie places a plate of scrambled eggs, bacon, and toast in front of me. "Eat. I was starving when I woke up this morning and have already eaten. After you finish, let's enjoy the day. All the boys are gone, so we girls can do whatever we want."

Her explanation makes sense. Mr. McMillan is polite, and it's not that he looks at me as some dirty old married men do at times. I feel like he thinks I'm lying about something. Then again, like Millie said, I'm being silly. He's nothing but pleasant. He even brought me to his home so I can figure out what to do next. If he thought I was trouble, I would still be at a local shelter.

As I stuff my face—Millie is a great cook—she sits next to me at the bar and sips her coffee.

"Katie, you want to go shopping with me and Hannah?"

"I'd love to." With only the five bucks I found in the bottom of my purse, I know I'll enjoy window shopping with them.

The fiver is all that's left of the twenty Roman gave me at the last game. I don't like going into the WAGS'—wives and girlfriends—suite where food and drink is catered. I feel so out of place. So he makes sure I have money to buy a sandwich and drink at the concession stand. I had forgotten to hand over his change, though he always tells me to keep it.

By the time we return from the mall, I own three shirts, two pairs of jeans, and a new pajama set. Millie insisted, saying that Roman can pay her back on his return. I argued in the dressing room, but then I noticed Hannah becoming upset, so I closed my mouth. I'll find a way to pay her back so she won't be embarrassed if Roman refuses. I'm not sure if he will, but I hate taking advantage of anyone. I don't know what to think. There is a possibility I'm wrong and he doesn't want anything to do with me.

One thing for sure is I need to find a job. Only I've never needed to work a job, and the few skills I have will get me arrested, except for my love of cooking.

Looking down at the new jeans and top, I'm quite aware of why she purchased the outfit. It has been a few years since I purchased clothes not designed to captivate a man's attention. As we went from store to store, more than a few men stopped and stared. Millie appeared uncomfortable with their leers and my barely-there shorts and suggestive skin-tight T-shirt with printing on the front that read, "Women Love Stick Handling."

Once I changed in the first store into something less suggestive and men quit acting stupid around me, the rest of the day went lovely and I enjoyed every moment.

"How's my girls?" Mr. McMillan walks in and hugs Millie and then Hannah. As crazy as it sounds, when he said *my girls*, my heart leaped. I kind of hoped he included me. Like in the father-to-older-daughter way, but I remain seated at the breakfast bar with a cordial smile on my face.

"Hey, Dad! Look at what Mom bought me." Hannah holds out her foot. While he admires her new shoes, I glance down and pretend to examine my fingernails, giving them a semi-private moment of daughter–father time. I notice one of my nails is broken and the enamel needs a touch up. I stand, planning to slip out of the kitchen to find my bottle of polish and emery board. They are still in my backpack on the floor in the bedroom upstairs. They remain packed since I have no idea how long I'll be here.

"If you two don't mind, I need a moment alone with Kitty...Katie." Mr. McMillan glances at his wife. She must've told him to call me that.

"You're not going to take her away, are you?" Hannah screws up her face as if she's going to cry.

She's so level-headed, I forget she's only fourteen. I want to hug her and say I'll see her again. But I have no idea what's about to happen and will hate to disappoint her.

"Hannah, go with your mom." His firm voice brooks no argument.

I wish I can go with her. His serious look tells me it's something not good. I slip my hands onto my lap to hide their shaking. *Please don't kick me out.* I cringe inside. No reason to keep being so needy. I'm a big girl and can find a way to take care of myself. I have since I was sixteen.

"Come on, sweetheart. Let's take these things up for Katie." Despite the smile on Millie's face, she gives me a worried look. She grabs the bags of clothes and playfully slaps one against Hannah's rear end.

Once they disappear upstairs, he says, "When I dropped by my office this afternoon, I had a message from Roman." He leans against the kitchen counter and crosses his arms. "He said for you to call him."

He hands me a sheet of paper with numbers on it. I feel his gaze on me as I open the yellow sheet and stare at it for a few moments. The writing blurs. My heart is pounding. The knowledge Roman wants to talk after being gone three days scares me as much as it excites me.

"What else did he say?" I ask.

"Nothing more."

"Can I borrow your phone?"

"You should wait. It's midnight there." He looks away and then back at me. "Whatever is between you two, is your business, but from what I've seen, he left you vulnerable and his agent took advantage. Roman owes you a good explanation."

He's right. I need to hear from Roman why he left me without a word.

"Okay. I'll call in the morning." With all the shopping and having fun with Millie and her daughter, I actually didn't dwell on my problems today. I needed the respite from all the worry about Roman and my future.

When I look up and see Hannah peeking at us between the bannisters, my heart lightens. I always wanted a sister. In the full day I've been here, I feel like I belong. Mentally, I shake my head. I know better than to believe that.

Whatever Roman has to say to me can wait one more night. Once I learn the truth, I suspect I might be expected to move on. Nothing like being kicked out of two houses in one week. It won't be the first time. I've survived before and will again.

Chapter 10

Roman

I wake to a vise on my head and someone winding it tighter. When have I become a wimp? Can I no longer handle my vodka? Shit.

My eyes stick together.

I use my thumb and forefinger to pry them apart. My lids easily slide up. Funny. I merely forgot how to open them.

The team has the morning off from practice and meetings. A good thing. After staying out all night, my aches and pains from the games have finally caught up with me. No Kitty to rub in some vitamin C cream. The hangover is just another discomfort to deal with.

With careful movements I roll over. I hit something solid. Not exactly hard. Reaching back with one hand, I touch soft parts. Oh, fuck. What have I done?

Since I walked out of my house, leaving Kitty behind, I've concentrated on hockey and certainly not other women. That's why I'm thinking of giving my right hand a name. Might as well be on a first name basis. So who the hell is in my bed?

I lean over and slowly pull back the sheet.

The honey blonde hair doesn't ring a bell. One of my Atlanta Edge T-shirts twisted around her waist reveals a glittery thong. Still no clue.

My cock is hard, but it is pretty much every morning. So I could've fucked her all night long and wake up this way.

Easing my leg out of the bed, I reach the floor and carefully maneuver around the clothes thrown on the floor until I reach the bathroom and close the door. I lean against it and close my grit-filled eyes. What have I done?

Damnit, did I cheat on Kitty last night?

I rub my eyes and face. What am I thinking? It's not like I asked Kitty to marry me or promised to be exclusive. We just haven't needed to look elsewhere for relief. Her sexual appetite is as strong as mine and her imagination even better. I groan and roll to face the door, thumping my forehead on the wood.

I release a line of curses. The slicing pain in my head reminds me of the hangover. I didn't need this. Then a flash of logic crosses my mind.

Kitty is in the States, and I'm in Russia. Nothing that went on at the nightclubs or in my hotel will be on TV in the U.S., if at all. So what are the chances she'll know?

The Internet. Fuck. I rub the bristles on my chin. She hates electronics. No problem there.

Feeling a little better, I take a shower. I need to get my act together, think of a way to get rid of the girl in my bed without a scene. No sooner than I turn off the water, I hear my phone ringing.

Fuck. What if the girl answers and it's Kitty calling? I asked her to call that number. How will I ever explain?

I scramble, yanking open the door, leaping across a chair as the girl looks up, arm stretched out, palm up.

"Some girl named Kitty asking for you." Her gaze drifts down and her big blue eyes widen. I hadn't grabbed a towel when I ran out of the bathroom. Naked and dripping on the carpet, I snatch it out of her hand.

"Kitty?"

"I called like you asked." Her soft voice brings a need from deep inside. My dick and balls begin to feel heavy. I turn my back to the woman watching me. No need to put on a show.

I squeeze my eyes shut and drop back my head, face toward the ceiling. I miss Kitty so much. I miss her sweet little voice, her gentle touch, her beautiful mouth around my dick.

"Roman?"

"Yes. Yes. Are you well?"

She doesn't answer and then I realize I spoke in Russian. I repeat it in English.

"I'm okay. Thank you."

Instead of the enthusiastic response I'm used to from her, she sounds forlorn. I'm not stupid. Kitty has told me her childhood was a drama-filled one, and she hates theatrics. For that reason she's the first woman to share my bed for more than a month, and she's been with me for a total of eight. Amazing.

I walk into the bathroom and shut the door. "Listen, the girl who answered, she's with Pavel." I cringe. Lying isn't something I feel comfortable with, but I keep making stupid, fucked up mistakes. I'll make it all up to her.

"Your old friend from Russia?"

"That's where I'm at."

"Yes. Ryan told me."

Relief relaxes my spine. She's talking to me. That has to be a good sign. Ryan is a good friend and will look after my girl without trying anything. If he does, I'll beat him to a bloody pulp.

"I'll be home in a few more days. We'll talk—"

"Got to go. Bye." Then the connection's gone.

Every curse word I know in two languages come out. My first instinct is to throw my phone against the wall. But, thankfully, I have better control of my temper. I need it to call her back.

I press the return number. It goes to voicemail and only gives a phone number. Whose phone is she using? It's not the same number for Coach. Fury wraps around my chest. I squeeze the phone, really wanting to throw it on the floor and stomp on it. I remind myself, if I broke it, I wouldn't be able call her back in about fifteen minutes. First, I need to get rid of the blonde in my bedroom.

Opening the bathroom door, I look toward the bed and around the room. She's gone. My T-shirt wadded in a ball on the floor. Getting rid of her was easier than I thought.

I dress and then stride down the hallway. "Pavel, you dickhead. Where are you?"

"Here. Where else will I be before noon?"

He's sitting at the kitchen table spooning in Cocoa Puffs. A buddy of his ships cases from the U.S. to Pavel. I curl my upper lip. I'm more of a Cap'n Crunch man. I shake my head. More important subjects to discuss than taste in cereal.

"The blonde in my bed. Did she and I...you know?" I jerk my chin up. "Shit, I feel like a drunken idiot. Did I fuck her?"

Pavel's head remains down with a full spoon hovering near his lips. "You kidding me? You don't know if you fucked her or not?"

"After we watched the replay of game one between

Nashville and Winnipeg, I remember saying I was leaving. I think I did."

"You did and the girl asked if she could share a ride."

"I don't remember that."

"She works at the club. Go and ask her after the game tonight."

"I will." I pull out a bottle of water. "I heard from Kitty finally."

"Did she tell you to go fuck yourself?" Pavel says with a mouthful of cereal.

"No, but we didn't talk long. She wasn't herself. So I'm still in deep shit."

"Hey, if you don't tell her, she won't know."

I tell him of the blonde answering the phone.

"Man, you're fucked."

In four hours, I'll be back on the rink. So I need to work at getting my mind on the ice and not with Kitty. I need to quit acting like a pussy and concentrate on my job. No more partying. Time to keep my mind on why I'm here. So far, my skating and points are on schedule. I'm getting a lot of notice. I'll try calling Kitty before I leave for the rink. We can apologize to each other. My head will be on straight then. Yeah. That will work.

She'll be happy with the results.

That niggling feeling tickles the back of my neck. I'm forgetting something. I hate that. To think of it, I had a bad feeling before I went partying. This situation I'm in with Kitty is probably part of the reason. Though I know ignoring this newest feeling will not be good, for the hell of me, I can't remember what I'm forgetting.

I pull out a loaf of bread to cut a few slices off to toast. I force my mind to return to the game last night and replay in my brain the good and bad things I did. Each time I replay the good plays, I think of Kitty and know if she'd been there, she would be celebrating. What is she doing? Why did she hang up on me?

Chapter 11

Kitty

I stare at the phone in my hand and it begins to go hazy. When it rings, I press the side button to quiet the sound.

"Oh, no. What did he say?" Millie places an arm around my shoulder. "Men sometimes can be so insensitive. Probably because of all the testosterone boiling inside. Not that it's a good excuse."

"He didn't say much," I say between swiping at my face and sniffling. No way will I tell her a woman answered his phone. How embarrassing. "He said he'll be home in a few days. I couldn't stand to listen to his excuse, so I hung up. He can tell me all about it when he returns."

Millie sighs and shakes her head. "Honey, I don't blame you. It's best to look them in the eye when they explain. Sometimes lies and truths get mixed up over the phone and don't get me started on email. That's the worst." She takes the phone out of my hand and steers me into the kitchen. "Let's have some ice cream. Everyone feels better after a bowl. You deserve it." She pulls out a chair and pushes me into it.

After pulling the tub out and dipping a good portion into a couple of robin-blue bowls, I place a spoonful in my mouth and sigh. She's a smart woman. The delicious cold chocolate hits the spot.

"Thanks, Millie, for the ice cream, for everything you've done. I'll leave this afternoon." I have no idea where I'll go, but I'll think of something. I can't stay here and impose on their family time. From past experiences, my presence alone can cause friction, and if it happens with them, I'll never forgive myself.

The clink of a spoon hitting the glass rim brought my gaze to hers.

"You are not." She takes a deep breath, probably realizing how harsh she sounded. "Guy and I talked about it. You stay here until Roman returns and straightens out his agent and apologizes to you. What you decide to do after that is up to you, but in the meanwhile, please stay here. I'll worry about you." She covers my hand and squeezes.

No one has ever acted as if they cared about me like she does and she barely knows me.

"Why? I'm a stranger to you." I search her face for the answer. The desire to be wanted raises up and I push it back down. No need to expect anything.

"Oh, honey, from the first time I met you, you made me think of my kids. I don't know. Maybe it's your brown eyes. They make me think of Micah, my middle child. He took his eyes after his dad. Funny, to think of it, you two could almost pass as brother and sister." She smiles and touches my chin. "Stay. Please. I want to be your friend. We women need to look out for each other, especially in this crazy world of alpha male hockey."

I really didn't want to leave yet, but I didn't want to be a burden. Without any money or plan to make it, short of walking the street, I need to find another way to support myself. I can't stand the thought of someone else touching me. So I'll lay off men for a while. It's all Roman's fault. No, that's not right. It's my fault for allowing myself to fall so deeply in love with him.

"On one condition," I say.

"What's that?" Millie tilts her head, curiosity shining out of her hazel eyes.

"Let me cook. I know so many recipes and I do enjoy cooking. I need to pull my weight here and I'll clean up afterwards." I give a big smile.

"That's a deal."

In a swirl of activity, Millie helps me pull food out of her fridge, bowls and pans from her cabinets. In minutes, I'm chopping vegetables and preparing the evening meal. A light feeling comes over me. Being with and cooking for Roman made me happy like this. Useful. I want to do the same for the family who took me in.

Millie proves her trust by leaving me alone while she picks up Hannah at hockey practice. She warns me Micah plans to return sometime soon. Her son's schedule uncertainty is due to a friend's car needing repairs before they can get back on the road.

While I'm working on the evening meal, the Russian girl's soft accented voice comes to mind. I wonder if she cooks for Roman. Food he's more familiar with like borscht? Or *zharkoye*? Is hers better? Does he make her feel special? Despite his claim the girl belongs to a friend, I can't imagine Pavel's girl answering Roman's phone.

"Hey, what's that delicious smell? I'm hungry." A tall, dark-headed teenager walks in. He's the spitting younger image of Mr. McMillan, including his dark, piercing eyes. "Who are you? Don't tell me Mom has hired a cook?"

His gaze slowly moves from my face to toes and back again. The typical look of a self-confident male checking out an interesting female. Nothing sleazy, more of an appreciative once-over for an older female. The flash of a big smile brought an answering one from me. Micah obviously preferred women, but not ones eight years older.

"Hi, I'm the stray that your mom and dad is helping out." I offer my hand. "Katie." It feels good to offer a more mature name as Millie suggested. Still me, but an adult version. "The food is *zharkoye*."

"Nice to meet you. I'm Micah. The lowly, neglected middle kid." The way his dark eyes light up, I know he's teasing. "So what are you making and how soon can we eat? I'm a growing boy, you know, and need substance. What's za-coy-whatever?" Considering he towers over me with his broad shoulders, I can't imagine anyone neglecting him.

"It's Russian beef stew," I say as he peeks into the pot on the stove.

"I've never heard of it, but I'm willing."

"My boyfriend taught me how to cook."

He feigns a heart attack. "A boyfriend? Now you've broken my heart. Tell me his name. Anyone I know?"

"Roman Volkov. Well, he was my boyfriend. I'm not sure what he is now." I blush as it sounds so stupid. What is he really to me? My ex? Everyone should have an opportunity to explain themselves, especially face-to-face.

Just as Micah is about to say something, his mom walks in. She squeals and hugs him tight, standing on her tiptoes to give her son kisses on both cheeks.

"I swear you have grown since I saw you last. You've met Katie? Of course, you have." She's smiling big, and he returns it. Though he doesn't have her coloring, the smile is all hers.

Turning my back to give them a moment alone, I begin to stir. These scenes of parent and child are what I always imagined most families did. When Hannah walks in and does the same, I know this family is real. They care for each other and are truly interested in each other's welfare. A sweet heaviness settles around my heart.

"What's all the hullabaloo going on in here?" Mr. McMillan enters the room and laughs. The look of pure happiness on his face as he clasps his son's shoulders and pulls him in tells it all. About the same height, but rail thin, Micah hugs his dad as if he's about to disappear. He laughs at something his dad says. The McMillan men are a sight to behold. In fact, the whole family could be in an ad for home life.

I've never felt so alone. Turning my back to the family, I busy myself by stirring the stew. The future I thought about with Roman flashes through my mind. A chill runs along my back. It's like seeing every dream I had go up in smoke.

No. I'm not going to feel sorry for myself. I level my shoulders and lift my chin. Taking one day at a time and appreciating the good things are important. That's how I live my life and will continue to do it. Alone but grateful for what I receive.

I place garlic and cheese bread in the oven and wait for it to brown.

"You can fix your plates and the bread will be ready by the time you're through." Though they don't stop talking, they move to the counter where I sat out the plates and utensils.

The next thirty minutes is filled with laughter and more talking. I bask in the excitement and love around me. They are so loving with each other and you can tell they really enjoy being around each other. As the late afternoon moves along, I begin to relax around Micah. For a teenager, he has his head on straight. The McMillan kids are so much like their parents.

"Hey, Katie, come in here. Micah is going to be on TV," Hannah shouts from the den.

I walk in to see the McMillan family piled on top of each other, laughing and teasing.

"They're talking about how he's the youngest on his team for his tier, and how he can block and out-skate his opponents."

"Cool." I sit in a comfortable chair a couple feet from one end nearest Millie and Micah.

"Come on. We won't bite and there is plenty of room on the sectional." Millie pats the long sofa. The three sections allow everyone plenty of room, though they appear to like to squeeze together. "Sit next to Micah."

He scoots closer to his mom and grins as if daring me to say no.

"Okay." I ease over to the end, keeping a few inches between us. The only affection I'm used to is the type leading to sex. So I have a hard time relaxing with such a demonstrative family.

My shoulders begin to relax when the sportscaster introduces his segment about Micah's team. About ten minutes into the program, Micah is interviewed, and they mention his famous dad. He handles the reference well as he wants to be recognized for his own abilities. We all clap at the end. He stands and bows so deeply he nearly falls over. We laugh so hard Hannah and I wipe tears from our eyes. I haven't laughed so much in years. I'm smiling up at Micah when out of the corner of my eye I catch Mr. McMillan staring oddly at me.

Embarrassed and unsure why, I rise to my feet.

"Anyone want a soda or water?" I always feel better moving or making others comfortable.

Mr. McMillan continues to watch me without saying a word.

The brother and sister stop their teasing and pipe up with their preferences. Such nice people. I make sure to keep my smile big. No need for them to wonder why their dad is making me feel uneasy.

His stare isn't a leer or anything dirty. It's almost like he's trying to piece together a puzzle, but it still makes me feel self-conscious. He probably doesn't even realize he's doing it.

I'm in the kitchen when Mr. McMillan joins me. I shoot a smile at him over my shoulder, trying to provoke the same relationship I possess with the rest of the family. Keeping a calm air I'm not feeling, I carefully pick up ice with the tongs stored in the freezer bin. I fill a glass and then the second one, waiting to hear what he has to say. Inside I'm trembling, but somehow my hands are steady when I pour in the sodas.

"I was wondering, where are you from?" His voice is flat as if he is asking about the weather.

"A little bit of everywhere, but until eight months ago, I lived in Nashville. I was there for two years, but most of my life was spent here actually." I don't have a problem answering questions. At least, he's trying to be friendly.

"So you grew up in Atlanta?"

"For the most part. When I was five, Mom followed a boyfriend to Atlanta when he was traded to the Braves."

"Your mom likes baseball?"

"Yes. She loves sports, especially men who play them." My grin changes to a sad smile.

I bet he's thinking I didn't fall far from the apple tree.

Only I make sure not to get pregnant. I've been lucky so far. The thought of having Roman's baby darts through my mind, and I quickly brush it off. That's never a happy ending for a person like me. The hard times Mom and I survived are not what I want for my child whenever I have one. Besides, Roman most likely has a girlfriend in Russia. From what I've seen of hockey players who come to the States, they usually look for a bride from their country. A tightening in my chest nearly brings me to my knees.

"Where did you live before moving to Atlanta?"

I blink at his question and then answer, "A little town called Mokena in Illinois. South of Chicago." Is he worried that I'm hiding something?

"I'm familiar with it."

Again he looks at me as if he's judging the truthfulness of what is coming out of my mouth. Everyone tells me the coach of the Atlanta Edge is a straight shooter. But I can't figure out what he's up to.

"Why all of the questions?"

"I'm just interested." He rubs the back of his neck, staring at his feet, and then looks my way again. His dark eyes piercing. "Your last name is your maiden name?" I nod. "Summerville?" I nod again."

"Yes." My eyes widen. "Do you know Elaine Summerville?"

His gaze settles on some spot above my head. For a few moments, a faraway look comes into his eyes. I guess I won't be getting an answer to my question. No surprise if he knew her. From the different pictures, plaques, and trophies, it is obvious he'd played for the Hawks in his younger days. Mom still watches every Hawks game.

I look at him and tilt my head.

His brown eyes are dark like mine. His hair color is

darker with the gray at his temples. His nose is straight like mine, but he probably had it fixed at one time. I don't know a skater with their original nose or teeth. He could easily pass as my dad. I mentally shake my head. There are millions of people with my eye and hair color. By the time I turned twelve, I stopped trying to find my dad in all the men Mom brought around. When I was sixteen, during a heated argument like teenagers can invoke, she let slip that I was stupid as my hockey playing father, but she still refused to give a name. Knowing my mom, she most likely had more than one man's DNA to consider. Anyway, there were and are plenty of dark-eyed, dark-haired hockey players. Don't I know it. As a teenager, I looked up on the Internet every hockey player in the Midwest.

If Mr. McMillan was my dad, he would have admitted before now, if not when I was born. He doesn't appear to be the type to ignore a kid of his. Not the way he cares for and treats his own.

"You better take those drinks to the kids before they lose their fizz." He lifts his chin toward the doorway. I nod, pick up the glasses, and walk down the small hallway back to the den.

Does he know who my dad might be? It would be nice to know. Not that I want the sperm-donor to do anything. Who wants to introduce an unknown twenty-four-year-old daughter to his family? Most men around my mom's age are married and even have grandchildren. What if the man was married when he and Mom hooked up? The wife would resent me.

It will be best not to ask Mr. McMillan any questions. I don't want to stir up trouble anywhere. Besides, in a few days I'll be gone.

Chapter 12

Roman

I call Kitty's number. No answer. Leaving a message isn't an option. I need to talk to her, hear her voice, hear the tone she uses. Everything will make more sense once she tells me what's really going on. After calling three more times, I decide to try my agent.

"Casey Perry here." The nasally voice causes me to cringe. I've never noticed the whine before.

"Roman here. Tell me again what happened to my girl." I understand Kitty believes she avoided Casey's advances by leaving, but it doesn't necessarily mean my agent came on to her. Maybe she misunderstood. Then again, I've seen how he talks to women. The man has no game.

"What is going on?" he snarls. "Your buddy, Ryan, and your coach, and now you're questioning me? I don't have time to play your skank's games. I have contracts to work on." His put-upon attitude is a familiar one. That's how I ended up with a shitty contract last time. Then it comes to me what he said.

"Wait, Coach McMillan called you? What did he want?"

"She's telling tales to everyone. She's trying to fuck with my reputation. I don't have time for her shit and that's what I told McMillan."

I lean back on my bed, shoulders pressing to the headboard, and stare at my phone. I can't believe this. The man is protesting too much. Deep in my gut I sense he's hiding something from me. Kitty is the least complaining woman I've ever been around. She doesn't expect anything from anyone. I'm more worried someone will...take advantage of her. Fuck. A light comes on in my brain. Kitty has never come on to any of my friends or teammates. She's polite and sweet, but slutty? No. Just to me and for me. All that sexiness she exudes is natural, but the naughtiness she saves for me. I've no reason to distrust her. Fuck. No wonder she wouldn't talk to me. Not just because of the blonde. I cringe with the thought.

"Listen you son of a bitch, you better be telling me the truth or your ass is fired. Got me?" I restrain myself from cursing in Russian too.

"What the hell, man? Where would you be without me? Playing the fourth line in some Midwest Podunk town, that's where. I got you noticed and a fucking good NHL contract and that's without you showing any of your limp dick moves you're doing now," he shouts. "How dare you believe that whoring bitch over me?"

I can see him in my mind's eye, his face red as he spits each word. But I remember his poor attitude toward Kitty. How dare he talk about my girl like that to me or anybody? If he'd been standing in front of me, I would've decked him.

"Well, I tell you what. Your ass is fired. And when I find out you harassed my girl, I'm coming after you, mother-fucker, and you won't know what hit you. Everyone will know what a scum bucket you truly are and you'll never deal with another NHL team." I cut off the phone in midstream of his cussing.

I can't believe I trusted that asshole. A lightness comes to my shoulders. I know it's the right decision to get rid of that scumbag. Now I have one more mistake to correct. I drop my phone and spear my fingers into my hair. I hope to all that's good in the world, namely Kitty, I haven't fucked up everything with her.

Chapter 13

Kitty

Throughout the night I wake up over and over again, my hand searching the mattress for the hard body I miss. By the time the sun is peeking over the mountains in the distance, I'm sore and stiff all over. Having another sexy dream about Roman isn't where my thoughts should be. I need to exercise. Sitting around and watching TV or standing in the kitchen preparing a meal for the McMillans isn't enough activity.

Roman and I occasionally worked out together. Granted, his exercises were more strenuous than mine. I like spending the time with him. Besides, I wanted his eyes to remain on me, and the way I loved to eat, running a few miles on a treadmill while he's there or not was worth it.

Like every professional athlete's residence I've been in, the McMillans have a fully equipped gym in their basement. Well-ventilated and brightly lit, it's wonderful. The large screen on the wall is great to watch TV, a movie, or to play an interactive game while riding one of the stationary bikes.

Over an hour later, I walk upstairs energized and ready

to shower. My borrowed bedroom is along the same hallway as Micah's and I hear him talking to someone as his door is cracked open.

"You have to do it. I can't. I barely know her and she'll think I'm trying to start something," Micah says.

"You're such a chicken." The sweet teasing voice is Hannah's.

"You know I'm right. It makes sense that you tell her. She'll appreciate hearing it from another female. You'd want to know, if it was you, right?"

Not wanting to be caught eavesdropping, I continue on and head for my shower. Probably nothing more than gossip about a friend of Hannah's from school.

When I exit the shower, a towel around my torso, I jump when I see Hannah sitting on the bed.

"Hey, sorry to scare you." Her smile quickly fades.

"It's okay. Just didn't hear you come in." After grabbing underwear from my bag, I step into the walk-in closet, leaving the door partially closed. Millie had made space for my few clothes on one of the rods.

"What's going on?" I raise my voice so she can hear.

Does she want to ask my advice about her friend? It will feel great to be treated like an older sister. With the life I've lived, I believe I can keep most teenagers from making the mistakes I did. Once I slip on my clothes, I return to sit next to her.

She sighs and looks at me.

I stay quiet, brushing my still damp hair, allowing her time to gather her thoughts.

"This morning Micah was checking out the scores for the tournament Roman's participating in. His team won six to one and now will play Canada for the gold."

"That's awesome." I'm so proud of Roman and how well

he's doing despite how he treated me. Though I'm still hurt about what he did, I can't shut off my feelings.

"Yeah." But she doesn't look happy. "After they announced the score, the program talked about their celebration." She sighs again and grimaces. "Kitty...uh...Katie, I don't know how to say it."

A sadness pulls at my entire body. "They showed him kissing or hanging onto a beautiful Russian model or someone who looks like one," I say, trying to help her spit it out. I'm not stupid. When Roman left without a word, he showed how little I mattered to him. Besides, there was the girl I spoke to on his phone.

"How did you know? Did you see it already?" The relief on her face helped me to say the rest.

"I suspected. A woman answered his cell phone yesterday. He claimed it was his friend's girlfriend, but why would she be answering his phone?" I said it more to straighten out my thoughts. I knew the truth but had ignored it to keep from being wounded more by Roman.

I try to smile but I'm sure I did a crappy job. Hannah's compassion is sweet. I brought this on myself. Expecting a man to take care of me. How do I keep from falling in love? How did my mom handle the constant pain from heartbreak?

"Can you show me the clip?" Talk about a glutton for punishment.

"I don't know." Her forehead crinkles.

"Please." I grasp my trembling fingers in my lap. "Maybe it's some form of self-flagellation, but I need to see it." Who knows, I might see something that'll prove it isn't what it seems. Maybe an act for the cameras? Deep inside I know I'm fooling myself.

Hannah drops her gaze and sighs again.

"Okay. Let me get Micah's laptop," she says.

She walks out and within a minute returns with the computer. A few clicks and a man with suit and tie is shown holding a microphone and speaking in Russian. A block of English captions run at the bottom of the screen, and I read he's talking about the great plays during the game. Hannah moves a small white arrowhead at the bottom, fast forwarding the video. Then the screen is full of partiers. The camera zooms in on a crowd of men, most of them tall and broad shouldered. The look on their faces is that of men who fought and came out on the right side with pride and determination.

Then it flicks over the men lifting their glasses and shouting toasts. No captions show up at this point. I recognize a word or two, but have no idea what they are saying. The camera moves to a dark corner for a few seconds. I can tell it's Roman, and a beautiful blonde is sitting on his lap, pressing her huge breasts to his chest. He's not looking at the woman, but his arm is around her waist, and he's grinning. I recognize that crooked grin. He's drunk. The woman kisses him, and he doesn't push her away.

My heart feels heavy in my chest. I'm sure it's trying to shrivel up.

I remind myself, we're not married. Not even engaged. He doesn't owe me his loyalty or celibacy. This isn't the first time I've been treated this way, but for some crazy reason I expected more from Roman. He is such a homebody on those few days he's not at a game or practice. He'd said several times how knowing his Kitty was waiting for him at home stopped him from hooking up. He'd claimed between hockey and me, he was a satisfied and happy man.

Of course, I'm no longer at his home.

Hannah stands and closes the laptop.

"I'm sorry, Kitty." She forgets to call me Katie. That is okay. Katie is another woman with dreams of becoming something more than a puck bunny.

"Can you pull up the last game so I can watch?" Maybe *I am* a masochist. I just want to see him skate one last time before I move on.

"Okay. Be sure to put it on Micah's dresser when you're through. He and Dad went somewhere." She opens it and shows me where to find the game. It's only highlights, but I'm okay with it as Roman is doing so well, he's in most of them.

A couple of hours later, I return Micah's computer and walk downstairs to the kitchen. I'm proud of how I haven't cried. For the last several days, I've shed quite a few in the middle of the night and more would be useless and redundant. Maybe I'm growing up.

I start dinner though it's too early but I need something to do. With the rainy weather, chili sounds good and the spicy flavor will get better as it simmers.

A friend of Hannah's arrives and they giggle all the way up the stairs. While I had exercised this morning, Millie had popped in and asked for me to keep an eye on the teenagers while she went shopping. It turns out school will be finished soon and then they are going to spend a month at a lake resort in Canada with one of Mr. McMillan's brothers and both families are coming to visit. All before he has to return to prepare for the drafts. At least, I have a deadline for when I need to find somewhere else to live.

My brain is swirling with everything happening. I'm scared. Where will I live?

.   .   .

Night has fallen, and half of the chili is gone, what with more of Hannah's friends dropping by and digging in. Millie had shown up an hour earlier apologizing for being gone so long and for eating a large lunch with some of the wives of the Edge. I wave her off. I understand. This is probably her last shot to see her friends for the summer. Besides, I have a feeling if any is left at midnight, the teenagers upstairs will lick the pot clean.

I'm amazed by the number of friends. Even a few of Micah's and Sam's came by checking on Micah. I had to tell them he was on an errand with his dad, and I had no idea when they'll return.

By nine, I'm dishing out ice cream to four chatting and laughing teenagers when I hear Mr. McMillan talking to his wife. I see them standing in the living room, whispering to each other.

"Hey, do I smell chili? I'm starving. Dad wouldn't stop anywhere." Micah walks into the kitchen. A couple of the girls say hello and giggle. He smiles big, and says hi back, but continues on to the stove.

"It is probably room temperature now. So you'll need to heat it up in the microwave." I hand him a bowl and spoon.

"Thanks." He looks at me, the smile still on his face, but there is something different. He's staring, not in his usual friendly way, more like studying me.

"What's wrong?" Wrong isn't the correct question. I'm lost in what to ask, but I leave it alone to see how he answers.

"Nothing." He twists his lips and stares into the pot, dipping out a portion. He refuses to look me in the eye again.

Something is going on.

At that time, Mr. McMillan and Millie walk in. Her face looks pale.

"Has something bad happened? Is Sam okay?" That's the only person not in the house who would upset the family so much.

"Katie, come over here and have a seat.' Mr. McMillan's voice is somber, but doesn't sound angry or terribly shaken.

I ease over to the table and pull out a chair. "I know I shouldn't have let Hannah invite so many friends, but they are being so good—"

He waves off my excuse.

"No. They're good kids. That's not what I want to talk to you about."

Carefully sitting down, I look at Millie and her husband. "Roman? Something happened to Roman?" My voice lowers, almost cracks at the end.

Hockey is a dangerous game. A stick, puck, blade hits the wrong place and a player is gone. Even a block can slam a player's head into the boards, and despite wearing a helmet can damage his brain or instantly kill him. Don't get me started on fighting.

Mr. McMillan shook his head. "No. I'm sorry if I worried you." He laces his fingers on top of the table, staring at them in deep thought.

My stomach is churning like crazy. He's going to tell me to leave. I'm so embarrassed. What have I done to merit being kicked out? There isn't anything I can think of that would upset the people I've grown to trust and admire in such a short time. No. I'm jumping the gun here. Time for me to chill and let him say whatever needs to be said, and I'll deal with it.

I silently release my held breath and uncurl my clenched fingers.

"I—I first need to ask you a few questions." He stops and waits for me to say something.

"Okay. Ask away." I have nothing to hide.

Surely they both know who and what I am. I'm a shallow puck bunny. I go from one hockey player to another whenever they become tired of me. Maybe that's it, Roman has asked him to make it clear he doesn't want me any longer. I brace myself for what he wants to know. I'll answer truthfully anything he asks. They've been so nice to me, I owe them that much.

"Has your mom ever told you anything about your dad?"

Well, that's not what I expected.

"Only that he's a hockey player and didn't want me. You know, not a son." I no longer feel dejected about the last part. The older you get, the thicker your skin gets. It is only a fact.

Mr. McMillan hisses and mumbles what sounds like "The vindictive bitch." He leans over the table and his gaze drills into mine. "She said that? That he didn't want you?"

His face flushes. Is he angry to think of men out in the world not wanting their own children, especially if it is a female? Mr. McMillan has shown how he's just as proud of Hannah as he is of his sons.

"Yes. That's why I didn't have a dad like other kids. Mom had a hard time until Ned came around. He's the baseball player Mom moved to Atlanta for. They lived together for several years."

"Your mom and Ned?"

I nod.

"Where were you?" Confusion crosses his face. Then his eyes narrow as I explain.

"When I was real young, I lived with a friend of mom's, Cecilia. Mom paid her to take care of me."

She was a bit of partier. From the time I was seven to twelve, I don't remember going to bed without music blaring. She loved football players, and I grew up understanding a lot of things other kids didn't about sex and the lifestyle of athletes. It was nothing to walk into the bathroom and see people having sex in the shower or against the vanity.

"Where did you go to school?"

"A lot of places. My mom's friend and Mom moved around. Cecilia's boyfriends were traded a couple times. The longest lasting boyfriend of Mom's, Ned, was traded after he'd been sent down to the minors. But he did great with the new team here. Atlanta."

"From what you told me and Millie the first night you were here, that you met Roman after your boyfriend had just broken up with you, I've heard it was Victor Lindberg."

"Yes." I'm feeling uncomfortable with this conversation. Before I can ask him to get to the point, he continues.

"You've been batted around a lot. For a person to have such an erratic childhood, it's amazing you're as levelheaded as you are." He gives me a half grin, but sadness is back in his eyes. "I'm not sure how to say this, but what if I told you I know who your father is? Would you want to know him?" His stare holds my own.

"I guess it would be nice to know, but it's not like he'll want to meet me."

"Why do you say that?"

"As long as I've been alive, I've never received a birthday card from him." I shrug. "Mom didn't believe in them either." His desolated look confuses me. So I try to cover the depressing statement with a happy story. "When I'd been living with Mom and Ned for a few months, he had some waiters sing Happy Birthday to me once. They brought me a cupcake with a lit candle on top. That was so awesome."

I don't mention it hadn't been my birthday. Ned often lied and claimed it was his or someone sitting with us. He was a bit of a cutup and thought it was hilarious. I liked him. I guess it was my turn. Ned had been the only boyfriend of Mom's to insist that I come to live with them.

I panic on seeing the stricken expression on Mr. McMillan's face. My gaze darts to Millie. She's gazing at him and patting his hand in sympathy and what appears to be encouragement. When I look back at the man across from me, he straightens his shoulders.

"Kitty... Katie, you're my daughter."

Chapter 14

Roman

"They what?"

I jump up, fists at my sides, sweat pouring off me in the *banya*. Steam loosens the muscles in my lower back from a hit I received the other night. Pavel is lying on the top bench with one leg raised for modesty's sake for the others. A Canadian has a towel over his groin and slaps a *venik* on his shoulders to cool off a little. Sitting across from us, two more skaters are relaxing naked with their arms strategically placed over their groins.

"I said a video has popped up on the Internet showing you with Nina." He adds, "The blonde." Pavel smirks and then howls with laughter on seeing my face.

"What are we doing on it?" I want to smash in his self-satisfied expression.

"She's merely sitting on your lap." He stands and stretches, laughing when the Canadian covers his eyes. Despite stripping and dressing in front of others before each game, the man's bashfulness is amusing. Only my attention is on Pavel's disturbing news. "Until she tongue fucks you."

I thread my fingers into my hair and pull.

"*Zalupa*, she was in my bed...with me...the next day. You never answered me the other day. Did I fuck her?" I whisper the last few words.

"How would I know? Remind me later, and I'll give you her number and you can ask her yourself, *dolboy'eb*." He slaps me on the back. "Come let's cool off in the pool."

I follow, uncaring how much an eyeful others get of my bare ass. One thing I miss about Kitty. Besides her loving to see my bare ass, she has a fondness for going around the house naked. The woman is comfortable in her own skin. The joy I receive in knowing I can touch her whenever and however and she's always willing to have sex. I've never met a woman as free and sensual.

If she'd been in the *banya*, she'd soak in every inch of the men surrounding her. And in turn, she'd never touch them or allow them to touch her. She'd proven time and time again she's all mine. Why hadn't I remembered that when I called her?

When I was a teenager and first came to the United States, I thought all American women were free with their bodies. It took several slaps and a few conversations from my coaches before I realized American women weren't exactly like I had heard. I must say once I earned a name for myself in hockey circles, women were free for the taking. Most were shallow, greedy and untrustworthy. In the beginning, I had thought Kitty was the same, but she quickly proved her loyalty and so much more.

The first time I realized she could be trusted was during a large party I held at my house. Of course, most of the team was there and several local celebrities: footballers—American and European—and baseball and basketball players, and a few actors and singers. I've found Americans party nearly as hard as any Russian.

Even Kitty was excited about the party, not only because it was the first we held as a couple, but the caterer had been impressed by her baking. He'd chosen to serve several of Kitty's dishes. For the last week, she'd been walking around with her head in the clouds, going on and on about Chef Paul this, Chef Paul that.

Six months ago...

"Chef Paul asked for a copy of my recipe for the pumpkin cupcakes. He was so surprised when I told him I don't write them down, but I told him how from memory. So he took up pen and paper without hesitation and wrote it down. He's such a sweetie." She leans over to where I sit and slides her tongue across my lips.

I fucking love it when she does that. Hell, I love it when she licks me anywhere, especially up and down my dick.

"So you're having a good time?"

I hadn't seen her for the past hour. From the sweet, spicy smell in her hair, she's been in the kitchen most of the time. The woman does enjoy cooking and Chef Paul rarely lets anyone but staff in the kitchen when he's working. Obviously, she's worked her magic on a man who has little interest in women. That's the only reason I'm not kicking his ass out of my house. I don't want her talking with such enthusiasm about another man. Yeah, I can be a little needy.

"Yes. Chef Paul showed me a couple dishes I think you'll like."

She crawls into my lap and snuggles her face beneath my chin and licks my neck.

With me being the host, I can't pick her up and take her to bed. I groan.

"Remind me not to throw another party during the season. Our one long weekend off and I'm giving up the chance to fuck you without stopping for three days."

She laughs and nips my chin.

"They all should be gone by lunchtime tomorrow. Then we can have fun all afternoon and evening." She wiggles and I harden.

"Hey, man, Casey is here looking for you." Ryan laughs. "You can fondle your lady later."

I help Kitty to her feet. She pouts a little until she sees the concern on my face and then she raises to her tiptoes and kisses me. The sweetest and sexiest kiss imaginable. As she walks away, I watch her pretty, denim-covered round ass. I adjust my dick so it's not so obvious when I follow Ryan out onto the patio.

Throughout the evening, I spot Kitty refilling drinks and offering different snacks to the inebriated in the hopes of sobering them. When I see a couple of the men flirt with her, she simply laughs and shakes her head. About three-thirty in the morning over half the guests have left, but there are plenty to keep the fun going. I hear shouting and then a loud crack. Like the sound of skin hitting skin. Fuck. The last thing we need is a fight. The coaches will get wind of it and we'll be in deep shit.

I run toward the direction the sound came from. Several men are shouting. Two are holding back another man. I don't remember his name, but he's an actor who has become a fan of the team.

"You stupid slut. When I get my hands on you—" One of my teammates, Connor Ellison, jerks his arm up, cutting off the dumb-ass's diatribe at Kitty.

Tears stream down her face, but the anger radiating off her body and from her dark eyes warn of her simmering outrage. Good thing Matt Linholm, a left winger, held her back. From the red palm print on the actor's cheek, she landed a powerful slap and appears to want to do it again. I've never seen Kitty mad. She's so fucking hot.

Returning my attention to the problem, I direct my question to Kitty. "What's going on here?"

The actor starts before she opens her mouth.

"The bitch slapped me. I'm just being friendly and she attacks me. You really need to be careful who you invite to your parties. The slut needs to know the pecking order here. She's been shaking her ass and rubbing up against everyone. I was just taking her up on her offer." The man jerks out of the hold. If Connor hadn't stepped back and loosened his grip, the dickhead would still be locked down.

"Kitty?" I say to her, while narrowing my eyes at the man for a second longer before turning to the woman living in my home.

Had she been flirting back? Is she a troublemaker?

A sadness flits across her face. I soften my expression. No need to frighten her into lying. If she's being too much of a tease or already looking for another keeper, then I need to know now. I don't share.

"Roman, can we go somewhere private?"

All the fight has gone from her. Her voice quivers and she looks at her feet. Though she's lived in my home for almost a couple of months, I've been on the road for half of that time. So I'm not sure if it is an act to gain my sympathy. My last girlfriend had used tears until I resented them every time they made an appearance.

I glance around. The few partiers still hanging around quietly watch for my reaction.

"Hey, everyone, Ryan went out and bought biscuits and sausages. The manager of a local deli is a buddy of his and came in extra early to prepare them for us. Go help yourself, and I'll join you in a few." My gaze stays on Kitty. She continues to stare at her feet.

"What are you going to do, let her suck you off as apology for making you look like a fucking fool?"

The man is getting on my last nerve. He needs to shut the fuck up. The dumb-ass has no idea how close I am to breaking his jaw. I don't need a lawsuit, but I certainly will ensure the bastard never comes to one of my parties again.

The actor is stupid or crazy for he crosses his arms and waits as if waiting to see how I punish Kitty.

I brush by her and grab a handful of his Hawaiian print shirt and haul him up until our noses almost touch.

"I beat men twice as big as you for a living." My accent deepens. "Your best interest to leave now, never set foot in my house again." Using the fistful of cloth, I shove him away. He stumbles, landing on the floor. I expect him to argue or even scream at me, but his eyes grow wide and he scrambles to his feet. Without another word, he turns and stomps toward the front door. The big pussy.

The room is now empty with the exception of Kitty. Arms around herself, she keeps her expression hidden from me.

"You have your privacy now. Tell me what happened." I step closer, gazing down at her. She takes a step back. I curse beneath my breath. Having her afraid of me isn't my intent. My voice comes out soft but firm. "Little kitten, tell me."

She finally lifts her chin. No tears on her cheeks, but her eyes are swimming in them.

"I was only being nice. Offering to refill drinks, seeing that everyone knew where the food was spread out, you know, pretending to be your hostess." She looks at me expectantly. I'm not sure what she wants me to say.

Instead I clench my jaw and then say, "You do understand, you're not hostess here." I have no idea why I feel a need to remind her of her place. Her reaction tells me it isn't what she hoped for.

Her big, brown eyes blink at me a couple of times and then she glances to the side as if she's coming to terms with the truth. She nods.

"I wanted your friends to like me," she says in a near whisper.

Cupping a cheek, I run my thumb over her soft skin. "That's kind, baby. Continue with what happened."

She bobs her head, pressing her cheek into my palm. Then she steps away.

"Tom came up to me and put his arm around my shoulder." Tom must be the asshole's name. "I stepped off to the side, but he held on." Her voice becomes faint. "He gripped my arm and squeezed. I tried to pull away, I told him he was hurting me. He said he'd treat me better than you. I said no. That you treat me real good and to leave me alone. He called me a tease. That I deserved to be fucked long and hard like a bitch in heat. I slapped him."

I grab a dainty wrist and push up the sleeve over one arm. Red finger prints, much larger than her own, are vivid against her creamy skin. Then I go to the other sleeve. Same.

It really only proves the dumb-ass had manhandled her. I look into her gaze.

The sadness in her eyes urges me to believe her, to protect her. During the few weeks of being together, she's been nothing but kindness and good-natured. Not once has she eyed another man with sexual interest. She complimented those around her, maybe even flirted, but not over much. She mentioned once she'd lived in the South most of her life. One thing I've become familiar with since being drafted by the Edge, Southerners flirted like most people breathed. Just part of their culture.

I wrap my arms around her. "He deserved that and more."

Her fingers dig into my chest. "Yes." Her cheek rubs against my shirt as she nods. "Thank you. I like staying with you. I'd never jeopardize my time with you, I swear."

She places a kiss over my heart.

"I enjoy having you here, but you must remember this isn't permanent."

My plans are to move on to one of the Original Six teams. So staying in Atlanta is not going to happen. Playing for an expansion team in a non-traditional hockey town wasn't my childhood dream. None of my plans include having an American female tagging along.

"However long you want me here, I'll stay," she whispers.

What a sweet, unwavering, selfless girl.

For being such a bastard, I don't know what I did to deserve her.

Chapter 15

Kitty

Mr. McMillan can wear all black with a kettle-shaped helmet and a bright red sword in hand while saying, "Katie, I'm your father," and I will be no more amazed and shocked than I am now.

"Why are you telling me that?" My face feels cold. I'm guessing I've gone pale.

Is he pulling a cruel prank on me? I didn't think he's the type. He has no idea when I was a kid I dreamed about finding my father. Then I woke up one day, sixteen and living with a man seventeen years older, and decided it was a waste of energy. If my dad wanted to know me, he should have looked for me when I still believed in Santa Claus and the tooth fairy.

I search his face for the truth. I really didn't look like him. He's tall and still slim and in shape even after being retired from the other side of the boards for many years. I'm short and have to watch every bite I put in mouth.

"Because it's the truth." He rubs his chin, the rasp of a five o'clock shadow. "I went to visit your mom."

For some reason, I'm not surprised he did.

"So she told you? When I was a kid, I asked her all the time. She never told me. And you never thought to look us up?"

I feel betrayed. First, my mom, Cecilia, Roman, and then the man I've grown to like and respect. The man who claims he's my dad. Why now? Why didn't he stay with my mom? People leave me all the time without looking back. What is it about me that makes people leave?

Gritting my teeth, I look away, not focusing on anything in the room. No need to cry about what cannot be changed. I learned years ago to go along with whatever other people wanted. It made my life so much easier. I inhale deeply. I'm happy to have a roof over my head and food in my stomach. I need to be grateful for the simple things.

"No. Your mother never told me she was pregnant with my child. Or any child for that matter. I haven't seen your mother since our time together, though I will admit to thinking and wondering about what happened to her." He leans over the table and rests his hand over mine. "If I had known you existed, I would've been part of your life. I swear it."

"Why didn't you know?" My voice comes out whiny like a child's, but I can't help it.

"From what your mom told me, when she found out she was carrying you, I had moved on and she had too. We were with each other only a couple weeks." His cheeks flushed. "I had just signed a multimillion dollar contract with the Hawks, and I didn't see her again after I moved to the Near North Side area of Chicago. I was young, full of myself, and careless with your mom. I'm so sorry, Katie." His sad eyes reveal the truth of what he's saying.

"Granted I have your dark eyes and hair, but we don't look alike. Why did you think I could be your kid?"

He shifts in his chair and pulls out his billfold from his back pocket. "This." He hands me a picture of a boy and girl grinning big and sitting next to each other. The boy is obviously the man in front of me. The smaller girl looks familiar, but I can't place her.

"The girl, one of your sisters?" Millie has told me he's one of six, three sisters and two brothers.

"Yes. Juliette. She's eighteen months younger than me. The first time I saw you, I thought how much you remind me of her."

Examining the picture again, I see the resemblance: the full lips, big brown eyes, and even the smile. That's why she looked familiar to me. A warmth spreads through me. Family. I have more than just my mom. Will they want to claim me too?

"Okay. Thank you for being honest with me." My smile trembles. I need time to come to terms with my new reality.

A knock brought our attention to the door leading into the den.

"Can I come in now?" Millie stands one foot in the kitchen with a hopeful look on her face.

I turn to look at Mr. McMillan.

He's watching me. "Up to you. She's excited about you being part of this family."

I swing back to Millie. "It doesn't bother you? You know, about me?" I ask with trepidation obvious in my voice.

"I will admit if I hadn't met you before, I'd be worried, but after spending the last few days with you, I think you make a perfect fit. Hannah and Micah already adore you and tell me how sweet and kind you are. I know Guy hopes you'll let him get to know you." She steps completely into the kitchen.

"Are you sure?" To me, Millie should be the framework for all moms. She loves her kids, cheers them on in whatever they do and hugs them when they hurt.

"Am I sure?" She hurries over to me, bends down to fold me into her arms. "Yes, I'm sure. I've seen the hungry look in your eyes whenever Guy and I have a family moment. Now you can be part of that. If that's okay with you? I don't want to push you. I want you to understand the invitation is open."

"Yes. If you think your kids don't mind?" I held my breath. Could a dream come true? Surely something will happen to take this from me.

"Of course not. Remember, they adore you. Sam hasn't even met you, but he's happy about it. He said it'll take all of the pressure off him in being the eldest McMillan kid," Millie says.

It doesn't bother me they had discussed it before Mr. McMillan told me. That's what real families should do, decide together what affects everyone. Being such a close family, there is no way I can keep my secret from them.

My heartbeat picks up speed to the point I'm afraid I will pass out.

Mr. McMillan and Millie laugh until they see the panic widening my eyes. Instantly they surround my chair, pulling me to my feet for a hug. I accept their affection because I know it's real. I never experienced anything like it.

As they stand back, letting me breathe from their enthusiastic display, darkness begins to surround me at the edges again. I have to ask.

"I know my mom said you are my father, but can we take a test to be sure." On seeing the frown on his face, I add, "Not that I don't want to be your daughter. I do. I'm so excited, but it all feels too good to be true. You know what I mean?"

His expression lightens as he nods. "Yeah. It will probably be for the best."

"I don't want someone to pop up and say they are my father or have Mom to change her mind." A squeezing around my heart tells me if I discover Mom lied, it will kill me.

"Whatever you want," Millie assures me. "I know whatever we find out, you'll be part of the family from here on out. Hannah already looks up to you."

I fight to keep the horror off my face. How can I be a role model for anyone? Do they truly not understand what I am? It's the reason I can be nothing more than a puck bunny.

Chapter 16

Roman

The plane lands hard, tires squealing with a couple of bumps.

Why aren't I one happy hockey player? I'm coming back with a gold medal and lots of interest from scouts for other U.S. and Canadian teams, including two of the Original Six that attended. The trip was a successful one. It achieved exactly what I planned. One drawback is since I fired my agent, I had to put the scouts off until I find another agent. Still, I'm okay with that. Again, why can't I feel smug about my success?

Kitty. I'm too worried about her. I need time to explain. For some crazy reason, Coach will not let me talk with her. I tried to get Ryan to mediate for me, but he said he was staying out of it. Staying out of what? Sure, I screwed up by leaving without talking with her, and I should have known my agent was a dog, and I still have to explain the blonde to her...oh, fuck.

I have so much to explain. I squeeze my eyes shut for a moment. She may never talk to me again.

My phone rings as I'm waiting for my luggage. Surely

this is Kitty calling. When I look at my phone, my smile fades at the name on the display.

"Hello, Papa." I answer in English. He claims it improves his American accent. Since moving to the States, he speaks Russian only every Thursday when he meets with a group of old men to play chess or *durak*.

"Roman, congratulations on your gold medal. I have been watching videos of you playing. Most exciting. Your brother tells this most important." For the next ten minutes as I direct the driver which luggage to pick up, Papa talks about how my older brother's medical practice has grown and how well Erik's children are doing in school.

I've learned many years ago not to worry with how Papa cannot see my success in hockey. Most parents would be proud to have a child playing in the NHL, the elite of the elite in a highly competitive sport. But it has always been Erik he's most proud of. The heart doctor. If my brother had been a douche bag, I would hate him, but he's always been most supportive of my career.

"I plan to visit you next week. I hope to see sweet young lady I miss out in meeting when I came to the symposium last January. She's been most polite for an American over the phone." He continues on about the rudeness and ignorance of those around him.

I half listen as I duck into the car's backseat while the driver loads my luggage into the trunk.

Halfway home, Papa finally tells me goodbye. That is when a light comes on inside...or is the American phrase above my head? Anyway, I realize the gold medal and attention I've been receiving from scouts is more to receive my father's respect than it is to receive the Edge's or Original Six's attention. Can this be true?

Nah. Papa plays a part, but not all. I'm losing my mind worrying about Kitty.

The whole time I was in Russia, I thought and stressed about Kitty. Not once did I think of my papa. With my mind on her, I have no idea how I played well enough to accomplish my objective.

I shake my head and rub at my temples in an effort to ease the headache building. I've done what is needed for my career sans any thought of my papa, but I should've thought about Kitty and her feelings. Though I'm not in love with her, she's important to my happiness. She does so much for me.

I need to figure out how to get her back into my house.

Two hours later, I open the front door to my home. The place smells musty from being closed up. My footsteps echo. I fucking hate how empty it feels without Kitty. Shit, I miss her happy face. I miss being greeted by the small whirlwind of a woman running and jumping into my arms as soon as I walk into the foyer. Or the times she surprised me naked and on her knees. My body trembles from the erotic image. She's the one who made my house a home. She's the reason I smile.

My chest is so tight from worry and need.

My cell phone vibrates. I pull it out of my pocket.

"Yeah?"

"Hey, man. You home yet?" From Ryan's tone, I'm guessing he's not calling to celebrate my medal.

"Just walked in the door. Why? What's up?" I drop my carry-on and leave the door open for the driver to deposit the other bags inside.

"You need to sit down. You're not going to believe me."

Oh, hell. "They're moving the team to Quebec City." I had been hearing rumors, but ignored them.

I nod to the driver as he walks out of the house and closes the door behind him. The tip will be included on the car service bill.

"No. Nothing about the team. It's Kitty."

I slump into a straight-back chair the decorator had insisted the foyer needed. Damn if the woman wasn't right.

"Is she well? Where is she?" I lean forward, elbows on knees, my free hand's fingers lightly massaging my forehead. If anything happened to her, I...I just don't know what I'll do. I need time to make things right.

"No, no. She's not hurt. She's Coach's daughter."

I pull the phone from my ear and look at the screen. Did I hear what I thought I heard?

"Say that again," I demand after returning it to my ear.

"From what I understand, they were talking one day and she told him her mother's name. He recognized it from a fling some years ago."

"Over twenty-four years," I add, though I'm certain this has to be some elaborate joke of Ryan's.

"Yeah. Her mother never bothered to contact Coach. She handed off her kid to a crazy friend while she followed a baseball player to California. When Kitty was ten, her mom showed up and brought her to Atlanta. Her last boyfriend loved kids and insisted Kitty come to live with her mom. Another baseball player. You've heard of Ned Whittaker? MVP for three years in a row. Good guy. No kids. He was crazy about Kitty's mom and wanted kids of his own. From what I heard, she didn't. They broke up. He died in a car accident a couple years back. He left a good chunk of money for Kitty and her mom. Her mom is the executor of the trust until Kitty turns twenty-five. It's enough that she could live without working the rest of her life if managed correctly." Ryan clears his throat.

Somehow the man always seems to know things no one else does. I guess that's why they made him captain.

Why didn't I know any of this about Kitty? I shake my head. Because she seldom talks about her life before coming to live with me. I've been wrapped up in my career and my goals and never asked.

"You still there, buddy?" Ryan asks.

"Yeah, yeah. I don't know what to say." I rub a hand over the stubble on my chin. "How did you find all of this out?"

"Coach. He asked me to tell you."

"Why?"

"Could be he thought you need to know what you're up against. The woman has to have trust issues. You know her past would scare off a lot of people."

"Not me." It feels right to say that.

When she turns twenty-five, she'll have money and no need for me. Damn. Did she say in one of her rambling chats she's a summer baby? So she will be rich soon with an equally rich father. Oh, fuck, that means her father is my head coach. No matter how I say it, it's any man's worst nightmare.

"She's still at McMillan's house. I'll text you the address. I finally got the house phone number too. The one from before was his office."

"Thanks, man." I have so much to do. Unpack and call a couple of agents who have left voicemails. They heard from the scouts I'm looking for a new one. The local news site and a few national sports reporters have asked for interviews.

Nevertheless, tired or not, the most important task...situation...is talking to Kitty and explaining everything.

"Glad to help. Let me know how it goes. You know, I never saw you happier than when you were with her."

"Yeah." What is there to say? The man knows me. "Thanks."

Then we hang up.

Ignoring my suitcases, I walk through to the garage. I unlock the wall key safe and take out the set I need for my Maserati. Kitty is crazy about the car. One time, I tried to teach her how to drive it, but she refused. She claimed she became turned on by watching me behind the steering wheel. Who can fight that?

I slide into the car and crank it up, allowing the engine to warm and the garage door to open. That's when I look at the clock on the far wall. Eight in the evening. I've been up for over twenty hours, but there is no way I can wait another day to talk with her.

Around a half hour later, I drive up to the front of the house, after convincing the guard at the gate to the community not to call ahead. Luckily, he's an Edge fan.

I knock on the front door. No one answers. I press the small lit doorbell. The chimes ring an old rock and roll tune. Heavy footsteps alert me someone is on the way.

Coach McMillan opens the door and blocks the way. I look over his shoulder trying to see if Kitty is nearby. No one.

"Hey, Coach. I need to talk to Kitty."

"I think it will be best you come back tomorrow at a decent time if you want to talk with my daughter." Then he closes the door in my face.

What the hell? I raise my fist to pound on the door, but I stop. Last thing I need is to make Coach angry at me. From the expression on his face, if I try anything, I won't see or talk to her tomorrow. That will not do.

Hell, I need to remember negotiations will be starting soon for my new contract. I like to think Coach won't let his personal life influence his recommendations to the GM. Do I want to take a chance?

I comb my hair with my fingers and stomp down the walkway and stop in the middle. What the fuck am I to do? What is going on? Ryan told me what happened, but Kitty claimed she had no idea who her dad was. I thought it was just talk when she claimed he was a hockey player. None of this makes sense.

I squint out at the lawn. Then I glance over to the house. Curtains flutter near the front door. The only thing left to do is go home, get a good night's rest, and return tomorrow. And find out where in the hell all of this craziness leaves me and Kitty.

I'm about to head toward my car as the sprinklers come on, water sprays me and my clothes. I glare at the front door.

What the fuck? Is this the exclamation point to the evening?

I trot to the car. Before jumping inside I shake like a dog, trying to rid myself of the excess water.

With another narrow-eyed look toward the house, I slip behind my steering wheel, mentally promising myself I will have my chance to explain to Kitty.

She's mine and nothing Coach can do will change that.

Chapter 17

Kitty

Peeking between the curtains, I watch Roman angrily stride toward his car after getting sprayed by the sprinklers. When he stops beneath the security light, shakes his body, I barely hold back a giggle. He turns to look at the house, I duck back a little, but he's not looking at the window. He's staring at the door with a glare that quickly changes to wonder as if trying to figure out what happened.

Mr. McMillan chuckles next to me. I can't believe he did that to one of his players.

"Are you sure we're right to do this?" I ask and then cover my mouth.

"A little water won't hurt him."

I grimace and say, "No. The waiting until tomorrow."

"He needs to learn how to treat you and not take you for granted." He looks over my shoulder.

"He's good to me." I peek around the curtains again and see the red taillights disappear down the road. My throat thickens as I struggle to swallow back tears. The need to be in his arms again tightens my insides. I miss him so.

"That's to be determined," Mr. McMillan says as he walks away. His tone questions the possibility.

Slim arms come around me and squeeze. "Something tells me he'll be back." Millie leans away and smiles down at me. "He must've come straight from the airport to be here so soon."

"No. He usually hires a car to take him to and from the airport. He's always worried something will happen to one of his cars in the public parking garage. The Maserati is his. He'd gone home and then came here."

"Well, I bet he didn't even unpack. Ryan said he would call and tell Roman where you're at so he won't worry."

I wrap my arms around her waist and hug back.

"Thank you. You always know the right thing to say." I turn and see Hannah standing at the bottom of the stairs.

"Want to watch some TV with me?" Hannah asks.

Her sweet question is motivated to help me get my mind off Roman. I hate to tell her that will be difficult, but worth a try. Her worried expression has me going against what I really want to do: beg someone to take me to Roman.

"Sure. Then you can help me decide what to wear when he comes tomorrow."

Her face lightens up. I look around and everyone is smiling, even Micah who has walked in from the kitchen munching a chicken leg. The boy cannot get enough to eat.

We watched several episodes of Hannah's favorite comedy. Then we searched through my growing pile of clothes. Millie promises to take me on another spending spree tomorrow, but this time with the money my mother released to me. Who knew I was rich? Well, not exactly yet, but will be in one more month. My birthday will be here before I know it, and she'll have to hand all of the funds over to me. Ned had been kinder to me than I had realized. How in the world will I take care of it? I know nothing about investing. Mr. McMillan—I'm still not comfortable with calling him Dad or even Guy—has mentioned about taking me to an investment consultant. That frightens me even more.

I wake early and start breakfast. By the time the bacon is crispy and coffee brewed, most of the family stumbles down the steps as they wipe sleep from their eyes. Only Mr. McMillan shows up alert and ready to tackle the day. In two days, school will be over and the family plans to start packing and leave not too long afterwards for their usual summer trip.

"Katie, my mom and dad, in fact, the whole crew, are looking forward to meeting you." Mr. McMillan pours a cup of coffee.

The grease pops as I move the last bacon strip toward a paper towel and spatters on my fingers. I hiss and jerk back, dropping the meat on the floor.

"Ouch. Sorry." I shake my hand and reach for another paper towel to clean up the mess.

"Are you okay?" Millie grabs my hand and pushes it beneath the faucet, running cold water over it.

"No. I mean, yes. I'm sure I'm fine. Just stings a little," I say.

As Millie gingerly picks up the hot slice, she glances to her husband. "You did not tell Katie that we want her to come with us?"

"I thought you told her," he says.

"Guy, I told you last night." Millie gives him a you've-got-to-be-kidding look.

My chest feels heavy. No, no, no, don't fight about me. The rest of the family will begin to resent me. My mind races with ways to stop the argument.

Mr. McMillan narrows his eyes and shakes his head, smiling. "Oh, hell, I was to tell her, wasn't I?"

I release the breath I held in and gave a silent sigh.

"Yes." Millie turns to me. "We would love for you to come with us. Guy's parents are lovely people, so laid back. They can't wait to meet you. Please say yes. His siblings are going to show up a few days later. We'll merge you into the family slowly." She gives me an encouraging smile.

Oh, my God. They already told his family about me? I have to meet people who will be staring at me, watching for similarities, expecting me to be smart and like, well, the man who had a part of making me. What if I disappoint them? What if I say the wrong thing? What if I embarrass him? What if they find out about...oh, no. I can't go, but I don't want to hurt his and Millie's feelings.

"I'll let you know after I talk with Roman today." Maybe this will hold them off. I want to be part of their family so much. I want to be normal, to love and be loved. When it comes to the man I love, I have no idea what our future holds or what I mean to him.

"You don't owe him anything." Before Millie opens her mouth again, the doorbell rings.

"Who in the hell is visiting this time of the morning?" Mr. McMillan pushes back his chair and stomps to the front door. I hear mumbling and steps coming back to the kitchen.

The glass of orange juice trembles in my hand when I see Roman standing in the doorway with Mr. McMillan watching near his shoulder.

Though I saw Roman last night, the artificial light had shown the tiredness pulling at his handsome face. He looks rested this morning, but something is different about him. Maybe a sadness in his eyes that hasn't been there before.

Yet, there are other changes since he's been away. His shoulders appear wider than usual. His hair is longer, curling around his neck. The short sleeves of his light blue shirt cut into his muscular biceps. Funny, he even seems taller.

I want to run into his arms and wrap myself around his body like I had during the months I lived with him.

"Hey, Kitty." He examines me from head to toe and nods as if satisfied with what he sees. His gaze softens. I've never seen him look at me like that.

"Hey." Tears well up in my eyes. All of my focus stays on Roman, causing everyone around me to disappear.

"She goes by Katie now," Hannah says from her spot at the table. Her chin stuck out as if to emphasize her seriousness.

Roman glances toward Hannah and then his gaze drifts around, taking in the family.

His attention returns to me, but before he can say anything, Mr. McMillan orders his family to the den with a nod. "Let's take our plates into the dining room and leave Katie and Roman alone to catch up."

He shoots a warning look at Roman as if to say, he will be far enough for us to have some privacy, but close enough to come running if I shout.

Once we are alone, Roman's brows rise. "Katie, huh?"

My face heats with embarrassment as I shrug.

"I needed a grownup name. They like me and want me to stick around. Did you hear that Mr. McMillan is my dad?" I shake my head in amazement. It still feels unreal. "Even Millie wants me to stay with them. Can you believe it? I'm part of a family. A real family. I never had one before." I hold back saying more. I know I'm sounding silly.

I bite on my bottom lip and peek up between my eyelashes. A puzzled expression crosses his face.

"You staying?" His accent is heavier. I'm not sure if it's from speaking his native language for so many days or if he's unleashing an emotion he cannot hold back any longer.

I point to a kitchen chair. "Let's sit and talk." We might as well be comfortable.

Before I take a seat, he grasps my arm and gracefully sits in the chair, pulling me onto his lap. The side of my face lands on his chest, and I sink into his warmth. I've missed hearing his heart beat, feeling his arms around me. We often sat this way before he left. He would tell me about his day or his trip.

"Kitty, why did you leave after I told you stay? I came back."

I sit up straight and glare at him. "You never told me to stay or anything. Casey said you told him to get rid of me. I know you don't believe—"

"Whoa. I never told the bastard to do that." He wipes the tears trickling down my cheeks. When did I start crying? "Oh, baby, don't. You break my heart." He reaches out but lets his hand drop. "I fired him. I told him over and over again to find you. After he kept putting me off, I knew something wrong." When I give him an incredulous look, he leans back. "I believe you. It's only right you do same for me. My note? Do you still have it?"

I slowly nod. "Yes, but I'd rather hear every word from you." My body begins to tremble. I have no idea where I put it, not that it will do any good.

"Fine. I wrote that I had to leave early and quickly. You don't have passport. One to Russia can take months, you couldn't go with me." Then he tells me about wanting to show the world he's a versatile, topline player. That he is more than a thug. With the gold medal and his stats, he has the proof now.

Such pride fills his face as he tells me about the trip and the accolades he's received in the hours he's been back. I'm proud of him. Unable to stop myself, I caress his cheek. He's more smart and talented than he even realizes. Me? I can cook a decent meal, and I'm pretty good at a blow job, but not much more. He can have so much better.

"What is the blonde to you?" I can't hold back any longer. I need to know.

He doesn't feign ignorance of what I'm talking about.

"I swear I didn't have sex with her. I didn't touch her."

No way can I sit in his lap and listen to this. I jump up and kick him in the shin.

"Ouch. What the hell was that for?" He rubs his leg and angrily stares at me.

"You're lying. I saw the picture on the Internet and the kiss, and she answered your phone and it was early in Moscow."

"She wanted a picture. She planted her butt on my lap before I could protest. The kiss, she thrust it on me. She stayed with Pavel."

"Yes. Big, bad hockey player can't handle a skinny blonde."

"Come on, Kitty. There hasn't been anyone but you." He stands and stalks me across the kitchen.

"I don't believe you. No way could you go that long without sex." I know my voice is becoming louder, but I can't stop it.

"I haven't fucked anyone since I left the States. The last person was you." His deep voice booms in the room though he lowers his voice at the end.

His big hands circle my upper arms, and he pulls me up

against his hard body. I'm a little afraid, but I'm also slightly turned on. Maybe I'm a wimp, but this is Roman. He has never physically hurt me in anger. Our experiments in impact play do not count; besides, it's too much of a turn-on. He caresses my back, and his hands slide down to my waist. My heartbeat picks up speed. He cups my ass and lifts me up to rub my pelvis against his cock.

"Hey, no shouting in my house. If there is any in my house, it will be me doing it." Mr. McMillan's icy tone from the other room causes Roman to release me and step back. "I think it will be best for you two to chill until tomorrow."

Roman's chest is heaving with emotion, but he dips his chin. "Fine." He looks down at me. "You need to come home."

"No. This is her home. She's staying here." Mr. McMillan marches into the kitchen and doesn't stop until he's almost toe-to-toe with Roman as he glowers. "If you want to see her, you need to ask her out on a date. Treat her the way she deserves. Get to know her."

I blink and watch the man I respect, and have begun to care for, act like a dad. I guess that's good since he's mine.

Roman stands a couple of inches taller than his coach. I can tell he wants to argue but thinks better of it.

"Yes, sir." Roman breaks their stare-off and looks at me. "Tomorrow is a gala the team participates in. Will you go with me?" His tone is so polite.

I can't remember ever being asked to go anywhere by anyone. I've always been told.

"Yes. I would like that."

"Good." He nods absentmindedly as if he's already working on plans for tomorrow. "I'll pick you up at seven."

Chapter 18

Roman

As promised, I picked up Kitty at seven. Now we're a block away from the gala and my Maserati is idling as we wait for our turn at the valet. I stare unseeing out the windshield with so many thoughts running through my head. What can I say? Deep inside I'm afraid of saying the wrong thing and losing her. I know that's the reason I keep replaying the last thirty minutes.

It was surreal to knock on my coach's door and then pace in his living room for my date to come downstairs. The whole time he stood by and glared my way. With his gaze burning a hole into me, I felt as if I was in one of the classic black-and-white movies I love to watch. Even as a teenager I've never picked up a girl at her home and certainly not at her parent's house. Sure, I escorted numerous women on my arm at what feels like hundreds of these things, but we met there or they spent the prior evening with me.

In the short time Kitty and I've been together, we attended only a few events as a couple. Most of the time, she begged to stay home, promising special food and sex if I let her. Who can turn that down? I liked showing her off, but I hadn't wanted her to feel uncomfortable. If the girl hated crowds, it would be cruel of me to press.

Thinking back, each time I attended an event, I would rush home to be with her instead of going out with my teammates. They teased me about being pussy-whipped, but I ignored them. If they knew the crazy and wild things that woman did to and for me they would be jealous. Ignorant asshats.

She often declared herself to be a homebody. I knew it was more to do with her lack of self-confidence. I complimented her looks, cooking, and the way she made me feel. Maybe I should have done more. Easy to see now, after I fucked up big time. I liked knowing she waited for me and the house wouldn't be empty. The last couple of days and especially nights have been torture being home without her. Most of my teammates would never believe it, but she is only the second woman to live full time with me since I turned eighteen and signed a lucrative contract with the Edge.

No one has lasted as long.

I glance over.

Except for the sound of the motor running and cars buzzing by, the interior is quiet. Kitty hasn't said a word since I opened the passenger door for her to slide in.

When she'd walked down the stairs at Coach's house, she'd taken my breath away. Her dress is some shimmering gold material and cut low in the front with a slit on one side showing a shapely leg when she moves. The color is perfect for her silky, smooth skin. Her big, brown eyes outlined in black set off her doe-eyed look. Everything about her heats me up.

So here we sit, not talking, and me with a semi-hard *khuy*.

She continues to face the passenger window. The reflection betrays her somber expression.

"You look beautiful tonight," I say.

"Thank you," she says softly.

"Are you still unhappy with me?" I open my mouth to say more but stop myself.

Hell, I should beg for her forgiveness. The whole time I was in Russia, I worried about losing her. Since my return, I'm finally near her and alone and stupidly struggle to find the right words. The connection we had before I left is there, weak, but not gone as I feared.

She has to see my side. My pride refuses to let me beg. A bad sensation crawls up my back. Am I foolish to allow my male ego to interfere?

"I'm not sure. Can we talk about it later? For now, it will be nice to see some of your friends. From what Mr. McMillan explained, the whole team supports the Wine and Cards Gala. It's nice how all of the money lost in cards and spent on the sports memorabilia in the auction is donated to various local charities. A small women's shelter I lived in for a while will benefit too."

"What?" I glance her way. My eyes narrow.

"While we're there, he and Millie promised to look for us at the Gala. He's a kind man. The whole family is." She babbles on with barely a breath in between. "He even offered to give me money to play cards, but I told him I don't gamble. So instead he insisted I tell him which item I want to bid on. If they have something from the Edge captain, I'm thinking of bidding on it. Ryan is a sweetheart and was so helpful while you were gone."

Why is she so nervous? When had she been in a

women's shelter? And what the hell is this about bidding on something of Ryan's? The bite of jealousy heats my face. A winning puck of mine is up for bid. The woman is going to drive me crazy.

Saving the question about Ryan for a better time, I urge, "Tell me about the shelter."

I hope to hell it hasn't been recently. Had someone forgot to tell me about that?

"When I was sixteen, Mom kicked me out of the house." She shrugs. "I had nowhere to go and asked a neighbor for help. She gave me directions to it. I stayed there for a couple weeks until I found someone to take me in."

Hoping the someone was a kindly older woman, I asked, "Who took you in?"

"Brad Johnson."

"Brad Johnson, Hall of Fame inductee, with Stanley Cup and two-time Ted Lindsay Award winner?"

In his heyday, he'd been a superstar hockey player who played with the Edge for a couple of years before retiring and returning to his hometown in Michigan. My stomach turns. He had a rep for liking them young. Doing a little math in my head, I fight back the urge to find the guy and knock his teeth down his throat. He'd been seventeen years older than her. She'd been a kid.

She nods.

"Sick bastard."

She nods again.

The line of cars in front of us move closer.

I can't think about what she put up with when she should be in high school and attending her first prom or whatever else I heard American girls do. Before I can change the subject by asking about Ryan, it's our turn at the valet station.

As I escort her down a red carpet, people take pictures as if we're movie stars. I don't mind, but I can tell Kitty is becoming anxious. So I rush her along, ignoring a couple of reporters when we enter the large arena. Panels cover the ice in the rink, making it into a regular floor. Different shapes and sizes of green-cloth tables for gambling are scattered over the attack-twice zone, and long tables on the opposite end have numerous items spread on top to bid on. Lastly, in the neutral zone are several bar setups, with tables blanketed with food.

As usual, servers thread through the crowd offering flutes of champagne—motivating people to lighten their billfolds. I grab two glasses and hand one to Kitty.

"I don't think I should drink this. I was too nervous to eat earlier." She looks around, probably for the McMillans.

"Let's go to the buffet." I want her attention on me. Before we take a step, I hear someone shout out my nickname.

"Hey, Vodka!" Connor Ellison, a teammate of mine, shouts and raises his glass. Almost everyone on the team has some type of nickname. Connor reveals mine with his teasing. "Welcome back!"

The man's already intoxicated, and the event started a mere twenty minutes earlier. Whenever he hits the ice, he's sober as a judge, but off, he drinks like a fish. His gaze lands on Kitty and roams over her breasts and legs.

I lift my glass, and move slightly in front of Kitty, trying to hold back my temper. When have I become so possessive?

"While you're visiting, I'll take my plate over to the

chairs near a bunch of ferns." Kitty takes a step toward a corner.

With the quick reflex I'm known for, I clasp her arm. "Give me a minute and I'll be with you."

"Sure." A confused look crosses her face.

From her expression, she knows it's out of character for me to hang around her during a party. What she doesn't understand is the old Roman is gone. The social butterfly has clipped wings. The new one is not about to let her out of sight, especially with Ryan Schmid walking in the door without a date.

My best friend struts over to us.

"What in the hell did you do to Kitty?" I ask without a care about my rudeness. My fists stay at my side. Barely.

"Roman, no." Kitty steps in front of me and touches my chest. "He only helped. People are staring." Kitty's soft voice warns.

I step around her.

"Well, congratulations to you." Ryan holds his hand out to shake mine. "From what I've heard your plans came to fruition. But why do I have a feeling you realize they aren't what you needed?" He drops his hand when I don't take it. A smirk grows on his face as I scowl at him. "And I didn't do anything to Kitty. That was all you, buddy."

With my palm flat, I slice the air. "Fuck you."

Kitty grabs my arm. I shake her off, almost knocking her down. On realizing what I did, I lean down and kiss her cheek.

"Step back, baby. This is between me and Ryan," I say softly.

Being the good girl she is, she moves away, shaking her head.

Returning my attention to the dickhead, I ask, "Tell me why you're trying to take my girl?

A glint came in Ryan's eyes. "You know I never heard you refer to her in the possessive. She deserves more than what you've been giving her."

A growl actually comes out of my throat. "I knew it. You want her for yourself."

"To be truthful, yes. But for some insane reason, she wants you. For that matter, she's in love with you. Like I tried to explain over the phone, she was scared. For you." He jabs his finger into my chest. His nose almost touching mine. "She came here trying to find out what happened to you. Your scumbag agent—"

"Former scumbag agent," I interrupt.

"Treated her worse than you did, if that's possible," Ryan finishes.

Before I even realize what I'm doing, my fist slams into his stomach. He bends over and coughs. Several hands grab at my arms and someone wraps a brawny arm around my neck to hold me in place. Everyone is shouting. A voice of authority breaks through the disturbance and I cringe. Coach McMillan. Shit. I've done it now.

"What is going on here?" When his angry gaze catches mine, he jerks his head toward the exit sign at the side of the rink. "Let's take it to the locker room. That means you too, Schmid."

As I follow Coach, I hear Connor say, "Hey, what do you expect, folks? All hockey players love to fight. Anytime we get together, we place a bet on who will swing first. Who won this time? No one? Then let's get back to the real gambling."

The lights brighten around the Edge logo in the ceiling as we walk into the room. Ryan and I head to our normal section of the bench. Ironically, we're sitting side by side.

"I'll start with the captain," Coach states. Arms crossed over his chest, he turns toward Ryan. "The man who should be a shining example of a cool head for our team. Tell me what the fuck were you two thinking?"

"Just a misunderstanding is all," Ryan says in his usual calm tone.

He didn't respond to my punch moments earlier, and he can easily rat me out. So *quid pro quo*. Besides, I know Coach will take pleasure in having an excuse to keep me from Kitty, deciding to follow Ryan's lead is an easy decision. He isn't captain for nothing, and he's still my friend. The bastard.

"Everything is cleared up now," I say, bobbing my head like a freaking doll. Where had my tough guy persona gone? During the time I was gone, missing and brooding about Kitty, I lost my balls. Lifting my chin, I wait to see if Coach wants to dig into our lies or not. Though I try to not stress about what Kitty is imagining, I want this to be over with so I can get back to her. Damn. There went my balls again.

His cold stare passes from Ryan to me and back to Ryan.

"I better not see this bullshit on the ice when the season starts back up."

"You won't, Coach," Ryan says.

"Not going to happen," I say at the same time.

Coach grunts and stares me down. "You and I will discuss this further later. I'll go and see if Kitty is okay."

I grit my teeth. If I didn't respect this man as much as I do, I'd tell him to mind his own fucking business. Only problem, Kitty is part of his family, and she's now his business.

How in the hell am I going to persuade her to come back home?

In an effort to regain my dignity, I stay after Ryan and Coach leave. I take a deep breath. Most of my life on the ice has also been spent in a locker room filled with sweat-soaked gear. Though the odor is repugnant, I take comfort in the familiar smell. My time on this team, in this big and wild city, has been a dream come true. I met the woman here in the U.S. who has become important to me. And for some idiotic reason I traveled thousands of miles to get scouts' and coaches' attention centered on me. Then I return to have the undivided attention of *the* head coach of my current team. All for the wrong reasons.

"Roman? Are you still here?"

The sweet voice whispering into the room belongs to Kitty. My shoulders slump, and I release a long string of curse words. Not from exasperation, but from knowing how much I missed that soft, feminine voice. I turn to watch her tiptoe in. She's so fucking cute when she does that. Like a little pixie. We're all alone and another thought comes to mind. A thought that proves I haven't grown up as much as I thought. I've never fucked in the place I love second best. The rink will have to wait for another time.

"I'm here, babe."

Her trembling smile betrays her worry. "Are you okay?"

"Fine. Come here."

She trots over and stops in front of me. I grab her hips and drag her between my legs. I lean over to rest my head against her breasts. She's built perfectly, soft all over. Her heartbeat picks up speed and reminds me of her enthusiasm in bed. The woman is amazing.

Her fingers comb back my hair. Neither of us move. I enjoy holding her like this, having her hands roaming all over my body. My shoulders loosen. Talk about soothing the savage beast, she has the gift.

"Are you sure you're okay?"

"Yeah. You feel so good. I've missed holding you." Damn, my voice even cracks a little at the end. I straighten my spine. My gaze searches her face.

"I missed you a lot too." Her dark eyes fill with emotion.

I'm unsure of how to read them. I just want to touch her.

I pull her down onto my lap, facing me. At the same time, I part her legs, one on each side of my hips. The slit of her dress makes it easy to bunch up above her hot pussy. I lean back against the wall behind me, so my hard cock can press against her silk-covered heat. She snuggles against my chest.

She feels like heaven. My fingers slide between us and wiggle between fabric and smooth pussy. I rub the hard nub, spreading the moisture her body provides. She pants as she grinds her pelvis against my hand.

"Please come home with me tonight," I plead in her hair and kiss the top of her head.

"We need to talk first." She groans and kisses my neck.

My shoulders stiffen. Damn, she's more like her father than she probably realizes. All this wanting to talk.

This is certainly not the time to think about him.

"In a moment." I fist her hair, carefully use the leverage to bring her mouth to meet mine. I nip her full bottom lip and run my tongue over it. Her eyes close as if she's savoring my taste. She moans and smiles.

She continues to shift back and forth against my hardness. I move my hand to a plump tit and squeeze over the glittery cloth. I love these beauties, perfect for my big hands.

"Baby, you feel so good. I need you. It's been so long."

For a moment, she hesitates. Have I said the wrong thing? She doesn't know how much she has me twisted up inside.

With a sexy smile, she lifts her mouth and I kiss her, diving in with all the pent up desire of over two weeks. Our tongues slip around each other's, and my need goes ballistic. The low cut of her dress is perfect for what I crave. I slip my hand in and massage the hard tip against my palm. With a flick of my nail over the sensitive end, she gasps, speeding up her movement against my length.

She sucks in my earlobe and then slides her tongue around the rim. My breathing becomes sharp, slivers of heat run down my neck and straight to my groin. Holding back isn't an option any longer. I push Kitty a little toward my knees to make room. In quick order, I unbuckle my belt, unhook and unzip my pants, and then pull out my cock.

The whimper from her mouth tells me she's as needy as I am.

I slip a finger beside the crotch of her panties and push to the side, nudging my cock into her slick pussy. I slide the head in while cupping her ass and then thrust hard and deep. Damn. The moisture, heat, and softness almost has me coming then and there. Kitty. She feels better than anyone I've ever had the pleasure of being inside. Something about the tightness and the way she squeezes my cock. Fucking good.

She tugs on my hair, silently begging for my kiss.

I oblige and plunge my tongue into her mouth, licking and sucking like I enjoy doing between her legs.

Lifting her hips and letting go so she can use gravity, I can power back into her pussy. We're grunting and moaning, not caring if anyone comes looking for us. Ending the wild kiss, I jerk down the top of her dress. Her tits pop out and I draw in a nipple while I pinch the other. She pumps up and down on my cock. Her fingers dig into my scalp. She relishes what I'm doing as her pussy squeezes and releases me in quick succession. I kiss my way to her shoulder and bite hard. She gives a closed-mouth scream in an effort to keep anyone from running in to check on us.

She's such a good girl.

Chapter 19

Kitty

I sit on the side of the bed and push my hair out of my face. Did I make the right decision last night? He acted as if he understood what I told him.

After the gala, when we were sitting in his car, preparing to leave, Roman placed his arm on the steering wheel and the other one against my headrest. His blue eyes searched mine.

"Go home with me."

My heart skips a beat. I want to say yes, badly, but need more time to make sure I'm not screwing up.

"I miss you. The house is empty without you," he implores.

How odd to hear him beg. For that matter, all evening he's been attentive and extra nice. He's never been mean. I must admit when he gives me orders in his deep, accented voice, I get chill bumps all over my body. The good kind. He expects instant obedience. Always before, I did whatever he said. Why not? I like making him happy.

I straighten my spine.

But I won't this time.

"Baby, go home with me please."

I melt.

Regaining my self-control, I tell myself to remain firm.

"No. Sorry, I have to go back."

Sure, I love Roman and want to be with him. But knowing I have a father who is willing to take me in, faults and all, I want to discover how it feels to have a family. A family who truly cares about my welfare. He has to understand. I need to do this to be a better person. How will I know what is normal and whether or not I can offer that to him too?

And I guess I haven't quite forgiven Roman for leaving me behind, leaving me helpless.

"Mr. McMillan asked for me to return home." One corner of my mouth turns up. It's wonderful to say home and know it means the word in all its entirety. "They also asked me to go with them to visit their...my relatives." I can no longer fight it and my smile broadens. "Can you believe it? I have grandparents, cousins, and three aunts and two uncles, even a great uncle. The uncles all played in the NHL. Wow. Who would ever guess?" I look at Roman's face. Though his grin encourages me, there is sadness in his eyes. I cover his hand on the headrest. "I'm sorry, but I want to go home to the McMillans."

"You haven't forgiven me," he says with certainty.

"Give me some time. I understand why you believed you needed to do it, but I was scared and all alone, worried to death about you. There's a lot I have to think about."

He looks at me for almost a full minute. I don't move, but I take the opportunity to examine the masculine face I love so much. Unable to resist, I caress his cheek with the back of my hand. I love his manly square jaw and the five o'clock shadow that always shows up before bedtime. He shaves in the morning and before bed.

Last January when his team was doing so good, he'd planned not to shave until they had the Stanley Cup. I had liked the beard, but the first round hadn't gone well for the Edge, and now his face is smooth.

A strong man in body and in spirit, he sometimes becomes wrapped up in the drive to improve his NHL level of playing. He forgets to look around and see how what he says or does affects those around him. I see that he realizes he's screwed up. By his current treatment of me and how he follows Mr. McMillan's conditions in an effort to see me, he's gone a long way in mending his errors. I'm just not at full forgiveness mode yet. I do still love him despite the way he deserted me and didn't consider my feelings in his decisions.

"Why don't you call him Dad?"

His question comes out of the blue. I think about it for a moment.

On catching his curious expression, I shrug and answer, "I think it's too soon. He hasn't asked and may feel uncomfortable having a stranger call him that. Even if he's okay, I'm not sure I'm ready. Anyway, I've never called anyone dad."

"You're wrong about him. He already acts like your dad."

"He's very protective of those weaker than he is." I duck my head. "The family has been so understanding and welcoming. I haven't...I've never experienced anything like it."

"Dads are important to a family," he states.

Remembering what he's told me about his father, I nod.

I figure most men like the idea of being a dad to a son.

Someone who they can help grow up to be their mirror image. Even Ned, who insisted I live with them, pushed me away after my body changed and I began to look like a girl.

Not that Ned was entirely to blame. My mom insinuated with ugly undertones that he paid too much attention to me. Though he denied it, his career couldn't take the suspicion hanging over his head. His morality clause would have seen him lose his job and any future in the MLB. So he began ignoring me. At least, he didn't send me away.

A couple of weeks before I turned sixteen, he walked out. Mom had refused his marriage proposal on the basis she didn't want any more kids. He became tired of her games and he wanted children of his own. From what I heard a couple years ago, he married but never had kids before the fatal car accident. Too sad. He would've been a great dad.

From what I've seen, Mr. McMillan is one. His interest in Hannah's life is equal to his sons. Nothing creepy, all rated G. Maybe because he's still so crazy about their mom. He appears to care for me, but too many years have gone by without his influence, and I'm no longer a kid. Millie may change her mind about me, and he'll change his. Then I'll be back where I was before. Alone. So for now, I'll enjoy each day with the family, and later, I can replay the memories.

"I'm finding that out."

Roman stares at me as if he never met me before and then without another word turns away and cranks the car.

In a way, he really doesn't know me. In the months we spent as a couple, the only questions he asked were, what are you cooking? What do you want to drink? Does this position feel better? The last one makes me smile. The man is an inventive lover.

One time in particular, I remember him asking for my favorite color. Then he brought home a dozen pink roses as an apology for staying out all night and not calling. He'd fallen asleep at Ryan's house. Our conversations consist of talking about his job, his friends, and family. I prefer it that way. Maybe I'm wrong, but I never want Roman to know the real me. Even now it's all tied in with the fear of rejection.

"I better take you to Coach's house. I don't want to be a healthy scratch at the beginning of the season because we're late." Roman grins and shifts his Maserati into drive.

"Did he give me a curfew?" A warm feeling washes over me. My smile grows. Considering how long I've been on my own, I should be insulted, but it's a great feeling to have someone to care if you're safe.

Roman glances my way. "You really like the McMillans."

"Yep. They are the best." I peek over and see his grim expression.

Did I say something wrong? I know he wants me to stay with him, but really, it'll be only as a fuck buddy. Nothing serious or permanent, but I need something solid, a forever man to love. Since staying with the McMillans and seeing their relationship with each other and their children, I realize that's what I want. Something real. Something loving and everlasting.

Always before, Roman avoided bringing up the future with me. And twice I overheard him say he's too young to marry and settle down. That he hasn't met the one.

I ignored the sadness that overcomes me whenever he says that. I must remember, I'm considered as nothing more than a puck bunny, someone to pass the time with between games.

With Roman, I'm happier being with him, and he appears to like being with me besides just sex. We get along wonderfully and have fun doing the same things during his off time. I can't remember how many of the classic movies we watched together and discussed afterwards.

But I'm not *the one* for him.

If I was, he wouldn't have left me without saying a word.

As soon as we arrive at the McMillans, he comes around and opens the door for me. His steps match mine as we move up the walkway, not so much to stretch our time together, but so I can keep up with his long stride. I stop in front of the door.

"Thank you for a fun evening." I bite my bottom lip to stop from laughing.

Feels odd to wait for him to kiss me good night. Considering having sex in the Edge's locker room is a memory I'll never forget. I feel as if I'm bouncing back and forth in a time capsule.

"I have to say I can mark it off my bucket list," he says.

We're obviously thinking about the same thing. He sweeps his thumb over my cheek and bends down. I close my eyes and lift my face. He kisses my forehead. Then he strides to his car without looking back.

I walk into the McMillan's living room, certain there's a confused look on my face. He kissed me on the forehead? On the freaking forehead?

As I think a little more about what he said, I'm not sure how I feel about being part of his bucket list. They are things you plan to do before you die.

"Honey, are you okay?" Millie stands up from the couch where she'd been reclining against Mr. McMillan. They are so cute.

I blink a couple of times. "Yes. I think I'll go to bed." I wave to Mr. McMillan and hug Millie. They say, "Goodnight" in unison, their expression clearly showing concern.

By the time I brush my teeth and pull on my pajama pants and an Edge t-shirt, I'm as baffled as I had been earlier. When I slip into my bed and rest my head on the pillow, I hear a light knock.

Without thought, I say, "Come in."

Millie shoves the door open and remains in the doorway.

I scoot up until my back is supported by the headboard. "Hey."

A few steps in, she leans against the dresser. "Sorry to disturb you, but I don't feel right letting you go to sleep without talking about whatever is bothering you. If I don't, I'll have nightmares." A brief smile crosses her face. "Is Roman putting pressure on you to return?"

She's so wonderful to worry. She could easily hate me for being who and what I am, but instead she welcomed me with open arms from the first day.

"He's asked. Actually pleaded, but I told him I need to think about it."

Millie's eyebrows lift. "Pleaded? Wow. He must realize he was wrong to treat you like he did."

"He says he does."

Moving across the room, she sits on the edge of the bed. "Do you mind me asking you something terribly personal?"

I can tell whatever she's thinking, it must be a doozy for sure.

"If I don't feel comfortable answering, I'll let you know."

"Okay. That's fair. Thanks." She fiddles with the lace edging on her pretty blue blouse and then wipes her hands down her jeans. "You're a sweet and smart girl. You could go to college and become anything you want. Or you could go to culinary school and become a chef. You're a great cook. How can I say this...sorry, but why do you want to follow in your mother's footsteps?" She squinted. "Sorry. I know I'm really not wording it right. I just want to understand why you settled for being a...." She flaps her hand in the air as if she can't find the right word.

I take pity on her and say, "A puck bunny?" I fight the grin wanting to break through. She's not hurting my feelings. I came to terms with my decision long ago.

"Yes, uh, no." She sighs, "I guess so. Though I don't think of you that way."

With a shrug, I glance up at the ceiling for a minute to gather my thoughts.

My words come out slowly. How can I explain why I'm okay with letting a man take care of me? Only I don't want to reveal everything.

"I guess growing up with my mother, it just seemed normal. I'm a big fan of hockey. It and baseball have been a big part of my life. I'm fascinated by the men who play the game, and they find me interesting."

"Don't you feel like Roman's using you? He'll probably continue to do so if you go back to him." Her voice is gentle, sounding protective too.

"You don't understand. Compared to the other men in my life, Roman is different. Sure he screwed up, but I love Roman. I've learned I'm the happiest when I make him happy."

"And you in turn receive money, jewelry, and a luxurious life." She says what so many others wrongly believed. Her face flushes in embarrassment. She's a kind lady and feels bad for vocalizing it. "With the way our fellows have to eat, drink, and dream hockey, we often come in second place. I guess in a way, we certainly deserve everything that comes with it," she quickly adds on.

"Yes, Roman has spent money on me, but I never ask for anything, especially money. Otherwise, he'll think I'm with him for monetary gain. The truth is, I want only one thing."

"What is that?" she whispers.

"Love. I want someone to love me. Completely and totally. I want to know how it is to feel cared for, to be loved, to be someone's whole world."

"You can stand up for yourself, improve your life without expecting a man's support, and still have someone love you."

"But that is me. I love making him happy."

"Certainly you have had a man to care deeply for you? To love you?"

"No. One came close, but I realized I was wrong."

"What happened?" Millie's gaze fills with sympathy.

"I woke one morning, and he'd disappeared." I glance over at the picture on the nightstand I had brought from his house. Roman is holding me in his arms before a practice. I'm looking up into his face. We're laughing so hard. Someone had remarked on our height difference, especially with his skates adding three inches to his six-two. We'd been together only a month at the time.

She covers her mouth and blinks in an effort to hold back the tears. Then she hugs me and I cry. For a person who never cried, I've cried more in the past weeks than most of my life.

Chapter 20

Roman

My plan to persuade Kitty to return home today blows up as soon as I hear a familiar voice yell, "*Moy khoroshiy*, where are you?"

"Papa?" I walk out of my kitchen, a cup of hot tea in my hand.

Sergei Mikhailovich Volkov shoves the front door wider and enters the house like a hurricane. He slings luggage into my foyer as he gives instructions to the hired driver.

"Place the other two cases next to my briefcase if you refuse to take them upstairs. For the amount of money I paid you, you should unpack and fix my dinner."

I squeeze my eyes shut for a moment. My papa falls short when it comes to diplomacy or manners for all that he claims to love the Southern American culture.

"Don't worry. I'll take them to your usual room," I offer before the driver decides to hit the old man.

"Where is *kotik*? Your cousins met your woman and said she's pretty and too good for you."

"Kitty's staying with her dad and will be back in a few days." I hope my words will help move his attention to other things. I'm not about to explain the situation with my father. "How is Erik?"

"Your brother is fine. Making lots of money off old, out-of-shape Americans who do not exercise and eat right."

For fifteen minutes, I hear about the money my brother makes—though I gross twice as much—and how his wife is beautiful and his children are so smart. The same every time I ask about them. When will I learn not to ask? I mentally shrug. It makes the old man happy, and I'm proud of my older brother too.

I walk into my den and exchange my cup for a shot glass, grabbing an extra for my father. I pour each glass full of vodka. During his stay, he'll mostly stick to beer, but a shot of Smirnoff as a welcome drink is a tradition in our family no matter the time of day.

Papa raises his glass. "*Za lyubov.*"

To love.

I lower mine and glare. "When have you become such a romantic?"

He throws the liquor down his throat before answering. "I've always believed in love. It is you who has forgotten."

Before I can say more about his sentimental toast, he heads toward the kitchen.

"Roman, are you going to feed me or do you plan to starve your dear papa?"

I slam back my drink and follow my father into the kitchen, rubbing my eyes to ward off the beginnings of a migraine.

Truly, I'm pleased to see him, but at times he can be a bit of a meddler. Since retiring and moving to the States, he has so much time on his hands, he takes joy in nosing into my business when he comes to visit. Last summer, he nagged about how the house is too big for one person, and I needed a woman to take care of me and my home. Chances are his remarks may have been the catalyst for me inviting Kitty to live with me. When I first came to the States, I went through women quickly, even allowed a couple to live with me for a short time. Then as I made more money, they became clingy and demanding. So I learned to kick them out after a few nights.

But not Kitty. She's different. Yeah, different enough that I wreck our relationship. I'm a freaky idiot.

I sigh and return my attention back to Papa.

"So what do you want to eat? Kitty has precooked several dishes I simply have to heat up." She's such a great cook, and often made so much she froze the excess.

Everything I offered to prepare or order in, he turns down. So we go out to the local steak house that makes the best breakfast. The place looks like a dump, but is crowded with a full parking lot and people standing around gossiping as they wait for an available table.

I see a few diners I know and we're stopped before being led to our seats. That's when I see Kitty. The whole family seated at a large round table in the corner. Their animated laughter and conversation easily showing their enjoyment in each other's company. Kitty's dark eyes glitter with pleasure. She looks so pretty in a deep-red dress with a modest neckline. Her hair is pulled back and tied with a matching ribbon at her neck. She looks to be young enough to be in high school.

I stare, wanting her attention on me and no one else. I've become obsessed with my kitten. No other woman has ever overtaken my mind as she has. She must return to my home, my bed soon. Or I'll do something stupid.

Before I know what I'm doing, I'm standing next to her and looking down, drinking in the many parts of her I miss.

Her slender neck is bare of the jewelry I bought for her. I crave to lick the tender skin beneath her chin. The delicate curve of her ear begs for my lips. Those big, beautiful eyes gaze into mine, and I barely hold off the urge to press kisses over the delicate, fluttering lids.

"Roman, it's good to see you."

I hear her words, but I'm unable to respond as too many sensations wash over me as I drink in her presence. My fingers ache from holding back.

How shocked would the patrons be if I picked her up and carried her out?

"Excuse my son. His mother and I tried to teach him manners, but too many hits to the head has slowed his mind. I'm Sergei Mikhailovich Volkov, this ill-mannered oaf's papa."

Then there is an explosion of chatter and chairs scraping against the old linoleum floor as the men stand to shake his hand. I barely observe Coach's oldest son is nearby. The eighteen-year-old is expected to be the NHL's number one draft pick this summer.

Sam McMillan takes my hand and starts to pump it.

"It's a pleasure to see you again, Mr. Volkov." The kid is grinning ear to ear and I automatically smile and say a few words. I respond with what I assume are appropriate answers. My gaze returns to Kitty. Anger flares inside of me. This kid can share her space, but I cannot.

A few more words are exchanged and then my father and I are back at our table.

"Roman. Roman." He snaps his fingers in front of my face. I blink and slowly bring my attention to his.

"Yes?"

"What is wrong with you? If you miss the woman, do as I did with your mother."

Moments go by before his words sink in and grab my attention.

"Kidnap her? Papa, I've heard the story about you and Mama countless times, but that was another time and country. No way can I get away with it here and now." Oh, hell, I'm actually thinking of doing it. I place my head into my hands and shake it in disbelief.

My mother's parents cared little for the young Sergei Mikhailovich Volkov from the wrong side of Moscow. He wore his hair too long and spoke in riddles about math that made no sense. As an unknown genius with little money and no prospects, their daughter had been forbidden to see him. My mother became a virtual prisoner in her own home. But no one came between Sergei and what he wanted. After planning and testing each step, he kidnapped the young woman he desired. His patience paid off and he stole the young Tamara. A week later, his future in-laws allowed them to marry.

"So what. I loved her so good that I ruined her for any other man in the first week. I fucked her until she was bowlegged and most satisfied."

"No, no, no. Please keep the details to yourself." I prefer to believe my kind and loving mother never indulged in such activities. She was a saint. "In the States, such will get me arrested and kicked out of the NHL. I would like to point out her father is my head coach."

"Roman, once he realizes how much you two are in love, he will forgive you." His hand waves in front of my face to punctuate the words.

My father is delusional.

"I care for her, but love? No." The way I feel has more to do with ownership, and I hunger for what we had before

I screwed up. I'm not through with her. "If she loves me, she would have never left."

I glance over at Kitty. She drops her gaze as I catch her looking my way. Her sweet shyness in public always causes me to be protective of her. I miss the taste of her skin, her tongue, her sweet pussy. I miss the sound of her whimpering as I slide my cock into her heat. I miss how her mouth fits around my hard length and her throat can take me to the end.

Fuck. I'm getting hard sitting at a table in the middle of a restaurant with my papa nearby. I'm as sick and delusional as he is, but he's right. She needs to come home and stay.

"If I do this, I'll need your help," I say.

"Good. Of course." A self-satisfied grin lights up my papa's face.

Chapter 21

Kitty

"Hey, Katie, where's your passport?" Millie walks into the bedroom as I slip into my jeans.

I've been dreading this question. They've been talking about the trip to Canada all week.

"Sorry, I don't have one. All I own is a social security card."

"No driver's license, student ID, nothing else?" Millie tilts her head as I shake my head. "Well, then. Let's start with that card. We'll need more to get you a passport. Wait, what about a copy of your birth certificate? Maybe we can use it too."

"Maybe my mom has a copy." My chances of having enough documentation to obtain a passport are slim.

I open my backpack and dump out torn jeans, tennis shoes with holes on the bottom, and other miscellaneous items I thought so important to bring with me when I ran out of Roman's house so many weeks ago. I finally come across my billfold. Looking up sheepishly from the mess I've made, I hand it to Millie. After my first day here, Millie had offered to clear out one of Sam's drawers, but I turned her down. So most of my new and pretty clothes Millie and Mr. McMillan have bought me hang in the closet or are stacked neatly on shelves next to the hangers.

Shaking the backpack again, all my old stuff spreads across the bed.

"What's this?" Mille picks up a sheet of paper and reads a few lines. "Did Roman write this?"

"I guess. He always left me notes. I save them. He's so sweet." The way she's looking at the note and then to me causes my nerves to jingle. What was written on it?

"You'd told me he'd disappeared without a word." Her forehead wrinkles.

"He did," I draw out each word.

"But you have his note." She waves the paper, bafflement clearly on her face.

I know what she's about to say as understanding dawns on her face. She knows, or at least suspects. How long did I really expect to get away with it? The only reason I could with Roman was because he thought of hockey and nothing else. I was only a way to relax, not worthy of an afterthought.

She sits next to me.

"Katie, do you have something to say?" She hands me the note. Her sweet concern will change when I tell her the truth.

"Oh, Millie, don't hate me." I stare down at it in my hand. The words jumble. My fingers ball up the paper.

I hold my shoulders up straight. Life has been hard on me at times, but I always bounce back. My throat tightens. I don't want to leave, but if they look at me with pity, I won't be able to take it.

She wraps an arm around me and squeezes.

"I could never hate you." Then she scoots back from me and gives me a stern look. "You probably don't know this, but I used to be a teacher until I married Guy. With all of the traveling, I quit to take care of my children though I still sub in if the district allows. During my time teaching, I learned the signs of a person being functionally illiterate. I've come across a few students with the same problem. You know, I wondered about your lack of a driver's license and never writing down recipes."

"I'm not stupid."

People have called me that and much worse for not being able to read. From all of the moving around with my mom's friend and then with my mom, I missed a lot of classes and learned to sit in the back and be quiet, be unnoticeable. About the time a teacher wanted to talk to my parent or guardian, we would move or I'd be out "sick." Then I stopped going to school at fifteen—the local schools had no idea I was in their area—and dropped out at sixteen. It wasn't like I was going to graduate anyway.

"No. To remember all the recipes like you do...no, you are certainly not stupid." Millie pats my knee and leans back. "You've proven to me how smart you really are. Hiding this for so long. I take it Roman didn't know since he wrote you a note about being gone a week or more, and he explained why he couldn't take you."

With shaking fingers, I cover my mouth. "That's what it said? He did tell me?" Millie's face blurs as I hold back my tears. "If only I had shown the note to someone. I could have done like I have before. Pretended I left my glasses somewhere."

"You wear glasses?"

"No, but it's a good excuse. People are always helpful." My cheeks heat.

I'm embarrassed enough without having to admit I can be dishonest about such things.

"Has none of your boyfriends questioned you about it?"

"Yes. One did. My first. He tried to help. That's why I'm pretty good at signing my name and my numbers. But then work got in the way and he lost interest." Actually, he was traded and hadn't taken me with him.

"I'll be happy to work with you. We can take it slow. First, there is a test I want you to take online. Don't look so worried. It's made specifically to find out how much you do know. Then we'll work an hour each morning before everyone wakes. After you get the hang of the basics, we can ease into longer sessions if you want."

"Okay." Relieved, I jump up and hug Millie. "Thank you, thank you. I appreciate that. It would be so awkward. I don't care if you tell them, but I'd rather the lessons be just you and me. I do want to read so badly." Out of the blue, I feel I need to share with her a tidbit about Roman. I guess I want Millie to think well of him. "Did you know Roman reads every morning before he begins practice?"

"No. Do you know what he likes?"

"Hockey." I laugh with her. "He always tells me about the books. Some are about getting your body in shape." I snort. "Like he needs help there. And others are about being mentally fit. The man is obsessed with being the best. Occasionally, he reads bios about..." I pause, "hockey players and coaches." I whisper the last.

"Of course." Millie throws back her head and laughs.

I join in and we discuss how she'll go about teaching me to read and write. Then I share with her about my time with my mom's friend and how Ned talked my mom into bringing me to live with them. I don't tell her about Mom's jealousy. No need to bring up such an uncomfortable subject. Don't want her to worry about something so wrong.

"Sorry to interrupt you, ladies, but you have a phone call, Katie." Mr. McMillan holds up his cell phone.

I smile up at him. Promptly, I catch the frown on his face. What has Roman said or done to make him unhappy?

"Thank you." I reach out.

"It's your mother," he says before handing the phone over.

Well, speak of the devil. When Mr. McMillan questioned my mom about me, he told her I was safe, living with his family. I never expected her to call or care.

My gaze darts over to Millie. Despite her encouraging smile, I feel the tension seep into every crevice and bone of my body.

"Hello, Mother."

"I need you to come to the house and sign some papers." No hello or how are you. I rest the phone against my ear.

"What papers?"

"Nothing for you to worry about. Just get over here quick so I can turn them in to my lawyers tomorrow."

Before I can think of what to say, she hangs up.

What is she up to now? I look at the phone as if it can give me the answer.

"What did she say?" Millie asks.

"She wants me to come by the house and sign some papers she plans to give to her lawyers, but she didn't tell me what."

"Does she know about what we discussed?"

I knew Millie is referring to my reading disability. "Yes."

"She'll certainly read them to you and explain before you sign them, right?"

"No. She's never been much for explanations." I shake my head.

"This is not the first time she got you to sign papers? And she didn't read them to you?"

I shake my head.

"That's just not right." Millie looks like she's ready to punch someone's lights out. The woman does have a soft heart. I bet she was a great teacher.

"What are you two talking about?" Mr. McMillan takes the phone out of my limp hand.

Millie looks at me, eyebrows raised, asking permission.

I nod. My secret is out. He deserves to know too. "Tell him while I get ready."

Giving Millie enough time to tell the whole story, I shower, dry my hair, and put on makeup. Choosing a pretty top to wear with my capris, I feel fortified enough to face my mother.

The expression on Mr. McMillan's face when I walk into the kitchen has me almost turning back. He looks ready to tear a person limb by limb.

"Guy, calm down and smile at Katie. You're scaring her." Before he can reply, Millie turns to me. "He's not mad at you. That's how he gets whenever he feels helpless. He hates that he didn't know."

"I can talk for myself." He gives us a gentle smile, wiping away the ferocious look. "I'll do whatever I can to help. That includes driving you over to your mom's to find out what she's up to."

By late afternoon, we pull into Mother's drive and exit the car, heading up the walkway. I feel weird. After swearing not to return, here I am without argument. Thankfully Mr. McMillan is with me. Without being told, I know he'll look after my best interest, whatever it is she wants signed.

She opens the front door before I have a chance to knock.

"You took your time getting here. How often have I bothered you to do a simple thing for me?" Not waiting for an answer and obviously not seeing Mr. McMillan a few steps behind me, she continues her tirade as she walks toward the back of the house expecting me to follow. She's dressed in a long, flowery lounging outfit; although a little dated, it's flattering. Being slender all her life, she's still lovely.

She faces me when we enter her den, and she points at a stack of papers on the coffee table.

Then she gives a frown over my shoulder.

"Oh, what are you doing here?' She finally sees Mr. McMillan.

"I want to see what you would like my daughter to sign."

"So she's now your daughter?"

"You never told me you were pregnant. It's not like I disappeared. I was still in Chicago and a couple million people knew where I hung out eighty-two evenings out of each year. So you didn't try to contact me. You never gave me a chance to be a father to Katie."

"Katie is what she's calling herself?" Mother asks, ignoring everything else Mr. McMillan said.

"Please. The past is where it belongs, over with and best forgotten," I say before more is said. I hope they will listen. "Do you still have my birth certificate in your safe? I need it, please."

Her gaze takes in my new outfit of a soft pink blouse with navy capris and strappy sandals. She appears to come to a decision, maybe believing if she cooperates with me, I will for her.

"Certainly." She walks to the desk and opens a false panel with a hidden safe. After a few clicking turns, she opens a thick door. She slides a folder and pulls out a thick sheet of paper and pushes it across the desk at me.

I exam the page. Though I can't make out the words, it looks official with a seal and all. One section is blank. I can only guess it's the section for father. I roll it and stick it into my purse.

"What is it you want me to sign?" I ask.

"Sign your name next to the red tags." She lifts the stack of papers and slaps them on top of the shining mahogany desk. "Then you can return to your daddy's house." The last sentence comes out in a sarcastic tone.

I touch Mr. McMillan's arm to stop him from saying the obvious.

"Mother, what are the papers for?"

"Just some legal stuff for when you turn twenty-five next month. Hard to believe I'm old enough to have a child your age. I don't look old enough." She hesitates.

Knowing her, she's probably waiting for me or Mr. McMillan to compliment her. Maybe it's spitefulness on my part, but I'm not in the mood to play her game. She's never been exactly motherly and compassionate to me.

The silence makes me uncomfortable. I duck my head so she can't see me roll my eyes when I cave. "You look way too young."

She simpers and flips her hair off her shoulder.

"Elaine, you haven't answered her." He picks up the papers. Mother steps closer and reaches for them, but he turns and walks away as he reads the top sheet. Then he comes to a standstill. He slowly looks up. "I won't let you get away with it."

"This is none of your business." She reaches for the papers again and Mr. McMillan holds them away from her. "Give it back to me." Elaine stomps her foot.

"What's going on?" I'm afraid my mother will cause trouble. Funny that I worry about a six-foot-one man being bullied by a five-foot-three woman, but she is famous for making life difficult for those around her.

"From what I'm reading, your mom is wanting you to hand over the trust fund Ned Whittaker set up for you when he died." Mr. McMillan shook his finger at Mom. "Stay back, Elaine. She's not going to sign it."

She grabs the papers out of his hands. One of the sheets rips. "Get out of my house." Her eyes narrow. "Now or I'll call the police."

"Karma is hell. One day, you'll regret doing your daughter wrong." Mr. McMillan glances my way. "Do you want to stay or go with me?"

"With you." I didn't have to think about it. In the time I've been with him, his wife, and their family, I've felt more love and kindness than I have in all the sporadic years I lived with the woman in front of me.

"Good," he says.

He walks toward the door, I'm a couple of steps behind. My mother slips into my path.

"You owe it to me," she spits out between gritted teeth.

Behind her, Mr. McMillan opens his mouth, but I shake my head.

"Mother, you know that's not true." She starts to argue and I hold my palm out to stop her. "Ned was a good man and you couldn't stand him paying attention to me. He never treated me in any way but as a father to a daughter. He treated me with respect. If he's given me money, then I'll keep it and help people like Ned did. You don't need it. Your last two lovers provided you great settlements. I remember hearing you brag about it. You always thought I was dumb and deaf."

"How can you talk to me like this? I need that money. All of it should've gone to me. I'm the one who did everything for him. You were just there, getting in the way." She bats her watery eyes at me and then Mr. McMillan. When she realizes we'll not be swayed, she marches to the door and opens it. "Then get out. I'll see you in court. That money is mine and I deserve it. You wait and see."

My throat constricts. I refuse to let her see me cry. She certainly has hammered the nail in the coffin of our relationship.

We walk out and she slams the door behind me.

"Katie, I'm sorry—"

"You have nothing to be sorry about. It's her. Not me, not you. No one owes her a dime or whatever. She's always been self-serving despite how often she tells others how much she sacrificed for me and the men who rotated around her. It's who she is. I need to move on and learn to live without her being a major part of my life."

Slinging an arm around my shoulders, he hugs me to his side and then we leisurely walk back to his car. We don't say another word until our seatbelts are locked and he shifts the car into reverse.

"Well, it appears you'll be rich on your birthday. You can keep on living with us or buy your own place. It's up to you to decide. Millie and I will stand by you."

What had I done to deserve such good people in my life? They make up for so much I had to deal with as a kid.

Unable to hold back the question I've been thinking

about since Roman brought it up, I turn to the man next to me. "Would it be okay with you and everyone if I called you dad?" I hold my breath as I wait for his answer.

He nods and meets my gaze for a second. I see his dark eyes shining. After clearing his throat, he says in a hoarse voice, "I'd like that a lot." He clears his throat again, struggling with his emotions. The big, tough hockey coach. "Millie was hoping you would and the kids have wondered what was stopping you."

I take in a deep breath and fight back the tears as I give him a big smile.

"Thanks, Dad."

Chapter 22

Roman

I want to hit someone. My fists open and close on the steering wheel as I stare sightlessly out my windshield.

For the last week, everyone and everything has conspired to keep me away from Kitty. I call each day and one of the McMillans provides a flimsy excuse like she's unavailable or in the shower. The worst is when no one answers.

The first day, I called to invite Kitty to participate with me in a team charity event, the Edge Fishing Tournament for Autism. Hannah informed me Kitty is afraid of boats and deep water and with good reason. She doesn't know how to swim.

Why didn't I know that? No wonder she always sat on the steps of the pool. I thought she did so because she didn't want to get her hair wet.

The second day, I met and signed with a new agent. Being the mover and shaker he claimed, he started negotiations with the Edge and that same evening arranged for me to meet with three sponsors. I'm now the proud representative of Robert's Foot Powder, a small company in Georgia. My agent said we need to start small and then the big dogs will be panting to sign me on. Big dogs? I like that. I like dogs. All ironic as my old asshole agent claimed I wasn't a big enough name to get a gig as a spokesperson.

By the time the third night rolled in and my evening was free, I was told by Mrs. McMillan that Katie was at the movies with the McMillan siblings.

I'm still not comfortable with my *kiska* being called Katie. Kitty suits her. She delights in rubbing up against me. She's soft to the touch. I'm happy she has a real family now, but I want my Kitty back. I want to prove to her I've changed, but I suspect she's avoiding me.

For two more nights, my obligations with my new agent and a couple of my teammates interfere with my plans to see her.

Finally, I receive a break from an unlikely source.

Sam McMillan answers the phone this morning. I can tell by his voice he feels sorry for me. Yeah, I'll take pity. I'm desperate. Whatever it takes to be with Kitty again.

He gives me a heads-up that she's going to a local skating rink this afternoon to watch Sam teach elementary kids the joy of playing hockey. He asks me to join in the fun.

Sounds like a good excuse to me. I agree. Besides, I like kids.

As soon as I hang up, the phone rings.

"Hey, Papa."

"This is...crazy phones. I still cannot get used to people knowing it's me. How's my Roman?"

"Good. I'm about to get ready and go to a rink and help some children learn how to play hockey."

"I see. How's the plans on kidnapping my future daughter-in-law?"

I shake my head. Ever since we talked about kidnapping Kitty, he's been pushing me to hurry. If he had it his way, Kitty would be living at the house, chained to my bed now.

"They have been keeping me away from her. It's as if they know what I plan. If all goes well, I'll see her this afternoon, and she'll be home with me tonight." Though I don't tell him the abduction will be a willing one if I have anything to do with it.

"Good, good. Call me if you need help. I have friends there who can help. A fellow I know called Savalas has connections with a nefarious gang—"

"No, Papa," I interrupt before I hear something I don't want to know. "You and your sketchy friends stay out of it. I will handle it."

"Fine. You were always independent." Someone in the background shouts Papa's name. "I have to go. Call me and let me know how it goes. Bye."

Shaking my head, I go into my bedroom to get ready to meet Sam. I'm excited. I will see my kitten today. She'll return and things will be as they were before.

An hour later, I walk into the rink with a wave at the ticket girl wearing an Edge jersey. She blushes and wiggles her fingers at me.

The class has already started. Around a dozen little eight- and nine-year-olds are shuffling across the ice, chasing pucks, sending them everywhere except into the smaller nets. I look around at the deserted seats until I come upon a group, mostly women, behind the twice-attack net. The parents. Off a little to the right is Kitty. She's dressed in a buttoned-up, pink sweater and her hair is pulled back in a high pony tail. Oh, she looks like a sexy high-schooler. Damn, she needs to wear that getup next time I'm alone with her. My heart picks up speed. She will.

Her gaze remains on her half-brother as she claps when one of the kids hits the puck correctly. As I'm about to walk over, a man stands in the middle of the crowd of women and moves over to sit next to Kitty. He says something with a big smile and offers her his hand. She laughs. Who the fuck is this *mudilo*?

I'm about to march over there to punch the man and break his pretty white teeth when I hear my name being called.

Sam McMillan is banging on the board with his stick.

"Hey, Roman! Come and meet the kids. They're so excited you agreed to help."

His big shit-eating grin tells me he knows what I'm looking at. When I step closer to the opened rink door, he laughs.

"Get your skates on and you can show them how you split the D with a dangle and scored after a nice deke. You know, like you did at the tournament in Russia. At the same time, you can show off for Katie."

So true the apple doesn't fall far from the tree. Guy McMillan's oldest boy can read me like a book. Hell, he has me thinking in American clichés.

"Only if you insist." I chuckle and sit on the players' bench to switch my boots for the skates I brought.

I peek over at Kitty every few seconds, trying not to be too obvious, as I lace up the skates. She looks so pretty. Then the asshole slides on the aluminum bench next to her, almost on her lap.

Pushing to my feet, I'm going to...do what? No way can I climb over the boards to attack the little bastard. My attention is jerked over to the excited, happy squeals coming from the kids. Sam has just told them I'm here to help. I grit my teeth and slap on a smile. The young ones need my attention, and they are so much fun, and Kitty isn't going anywhere. She'd ridden in with Sam and will be leaving with me.

For the next hour, I enjoy the hell out of the time with Sam and his students. The big McMillan kid has talent and a feel for the ice. I've watched several of his college games on TV. He senses how the puck will go by the way the player holds his stick. Few players have that ability.

Goofing off with the kids, we decide to end the time with slap-shots to the nets. One shot spins and deflects on the pipes into the seats. I swear I didn't purposely do it. Fuck, how was I to know the protective netting needed patching in that area? Maybe it's a sign. The dumbass sitting next to Kitty didn't even duck. The biscuit ricochets off his forehead. Pure luck that the angle of the hit saves him from being knocked out. Sam hollers for the manager of the rink. Within five minutes, they're hauling off the man to the nearest emergency facility for an x-ray.

"Don't tell me you did that on purpose." Kitty walks up to the bench where I'm unlacing my skates.

I lift my eyebrows as if to say, who me? Several of the kids skate by chattering away about the mishap. They hold up their hands for me to slap as they pass.

A few seconds go by as I slip out of my skates and then tug on my boots.

"No. I didn't." While I tie the laces together to make it easier to carry the pair, I can't resist grinning at her.

"Roman," she says with reproach.

"Would I do such a thing?" I ask with eyes wide, trying for an innocent look. "I swear I didn't."

She watches me for a few seconds. "I'm glad. He's a nice person." Jealousy zips through me. "It's good seeing you today." She leans over and kisses my cheek.

My heartbeat picks up speed. I almost can't breathe. My cock perks up. I loop an arm around her waist and bring her down onto my lap and give a slight thrust. Just enough for her to feel my reaction. No need to give the kids a sex education class today. I hear young giggles in the background.

I lightly kiss her lips and lean back. "Come home with me. I miss you, *kotyonok*." All of my patience is in those words. I wanted to snatch her up against my chest and walk out, leaving everyone behind.

"Sorry. I promised to prepare dinner tonight. Since we're having problems getting me a passport, they decided to wait a few days. The lawyer said he should be able to pull some strings. Just think, I'll be able to meet my extended family in Canada. I have *extended* family. In Canada. Can you believe it?" Her sweet face brightens with each word.

"I'm happy for you." I give her a big smile, despite how much I feel like I'm losing her. My heart pounds with fear of never seeing her again. I hoped to have more time. Damn, I want her to stay with me, for her to want to stay with me.

She caresses my face from temple to chin.

"Don't worry. I'll be back and you can ask me out on another date." She kisses the tip of my nose. I scowl. No way can I hide how I feel about *dating*. Dating fucking sucks. "Don't look like that. It's nice to be a normal person."

Normal?

"What do you mean by normal?" My gaze scans her body up and down. "You..." I wave my hand down her body, "are better than normal."

"You're so sweet. As in having you pick me up and take me out for dinner and a movie. Growing up without a dad to look after me, and having a mom who...well, she's different from Millie. Millie's like a TV mom. Anyway, I never had anyone to look out for me like my dad does now. He and Millie care about me."

"I care about you. A lot." I want to say more, but this isn't the right time.

Her smile fades as she becomes serious. "I wasn't always sure of that. You were fun and so sexy." Those dark eyes soften. "But I never felt as if I mattered to you."

Before I can respond, I hear the shuffle of feet.

"You ready," Sam says to Kitty as he nods toward the doors.

"I'm taking her home." My tone brooks no argument.

"You don't mind?" Sam waits for her answer.

She sighs. "Go on. I'll see you at home."

"See you later, Sis." Sam gives her a crooked grin.

Her whole countenance shines with pleasure. She likes what he called her. Her eyes even smile.

I remember many times she laughed with me, but her eyes remained sad. Why did I let those moments go by without asking her what was wrong?

I know why.

I'm a self-centered prick.

As I place my arm around her waist and usher her out to my car, I realize what I'm about to do classifies me as a big, self-centered asshole.

Chapter 23

Kitty

I scoot down further into the soft leather interior of Roman's Maserati. Resting my cheek against the back of the seat, I check out the tall, muscular Russian. How in the world had I forgotten how sexy he looks behind the wheel of the powerful car? Biceps swelling and releasing each time he turns the steering wheel. Chest muscles bunching and relaxing with his movements. I'm fascinated by how every inch of his body moves. He told me the car drives like a dream, and like everything he does in his life, he puts his all into driving efficiently and safely.

In the rink, his safety gear and loose uniform deceives a person into believing he's bulky and out of shape. Looking at baseball and football players in their skin-tight uniforms and basketball players in their thin ones, you can easily see hard muscles. People don't realize how strong and toned all over an NHL skater must be to perform his job. Though it only takes watching Roman's footwork and stick handling to know the man is physically fit.

Speaking of baseball players...

"Guess what I found out a few days ago." I'm excited,

but unsure how he'll take it. Will his pride get in the way if he knows I'm rich too? It will be nice to have money he hasn't given me that I can spend.

"What's that?" He glances over and skims his palm over my knee.

My eyes partially close with a silent sigh as I melt into the seat. The warmth of his big hand reminds me what I've been missing. The quickie in the locker room too many days ago wasn't enough.

Regaining my composure, I answer. "I've found out Mr. Whittaker left me a trust. When I turn twenty-five, I get to take control of it. He was such a nice man." My voice cracks a little on the last word. I'm such a bundle of nerves and emotions lately. "I wish I had a chance to tell him thank you."

"Yes, I heard about your good fortune," Roman replies, his gaze remaining on the road.

"Who told you?"

His whole body tenses as guilt spreads across his face. What is wrong with this man that he continues to hide so much from me? Why can't he be upfront?

"I had a tech-savvy friend do a search on the internet."

"So like many other things, everyone knew but me?" I don't know how I should feel about his admission.

"No, this was after you found out. He came across an old article online about Whittaker's death. Did no one ever show you the article?"

It was my time to feel guilty.

Inhaling deeply to fortify myself, I finally admit my secret. "Roman, I can't read."

He's quiet as he takes the exit off the interstate.

"Did you hear me?"

"So my note I left you, you never read it?" His forehead wrinkles in confusion.

"No. I didn't. I couldn't. I didn't know how."

"All the times I left you notes and you claimed you didn't see them or they disappeared, they were excuses?"

"I'm sorry—"

He holds up his hand to stop my apology.

"What Coach told me about what happened to you with Casey, was it true?"

Does he feel betrayed by my hiding something so big? So is he going to doubt everything I say?

"Yes. I had no reason to lie about that." Going back to the note, I add, "I didn't know what you said in the note, I swear, until Millie read it. That's how she figured out I couldn't read. That's why I'm telling you. I can't keep it hidden any longer, and whoever told you stuff about me, well, I didn't want you to find out that way." I take a deep breath. Then something he said gets me to thinking. "Did you tell Casey you left a note?"

"I did."

"He must have guessed I didn't know how to read."

"It appears so." His deep, thoughtful tone pulls my attention to him.

"What are you thinking?"

"I'm thinking I'm stupid. In just under three weeks, the McMillans figure out you can't read. With a simple Google search, a friend can find out more about you than I've ever known. I want to change that. The best way for me to know you is to stop everyone from interfering in our lives."

That's when I notice we're passing a familiar street. We're not on the road back to Coach's house.

"Where are we going?" As soon as the words are out of my mouth I recognize the neighborhood. "Why are we going to your home? I—I have to go back to the McMillians'. I promised to cook tonight." Why did Roman lie to me? Why is he driving me here? "You said you'll take me home."

"This is your home. We need a little alone time to straighten everything out, Kitty."

"No. This is not my home, and my name is Katie now. I prefer that name." Deep inside it hurts to say the last. I do love the way he says Kitty, but I have to make Roman understand we cannot go back to the way it was before.

"Did I ever tell you that my mother was engaged to another man when my papa met her?"

As soon as he pulls into his garage, the large door lowers behind us. This is worrying me. His obstinate attitude does not help smooth matters at all.

"What's that have to do with you refusing to take me to the McMillan's? I'm not engaged to you or anyone." Obstinacy appears to be contagious.

He ignores my comment and continues, "He had met her at a friend's house the month before. Being a young mathematician making news with a couple of his racial theories, he was a bit of an intellect superstar at the time. Women love men with big brains too."

He raises his eyebrows, obviously wanting me to laugh at his comment.

I merely stare back. His stubbornness is scary. Though I know he will never physically harm me, it doesn't mean he won't lock me up and keep me from my new-found family.

He shrugs and then says, "They flocked to him. He could have all the pussy he wanted."

"I *so* didn't need to hear that." From the times I've talked with his dad over the phone, I imagine he charmed many women in his heyday and from what I saw at the restaurant he continues to do so. He's a well-formed and nice looking man.

"After he met my mother, he had no interest in any of the women who wanted in his bed. He was going insane thinking only of her."

"That kind of sounds sad."

"It is. To have your thoughts on a person who became your one and only, and to not know if she feels the same." Is he talking about us? I don't believe it. "You must understand, it can be most disturbing. So he kidnapped her and took her to friend's country home. They spent many heated nights." His accent deepens.

Does he think I believe this is romantic? Maybe it would be nice to have someone care so much, but to force himself on her. At least, that's the impression I get. "I'm surprised she ever had anything to do with him after that."

"She fell in love. It turned out she didn't want to marry the other man. She'd fallen for Papa too. My brother was born nine months later."

"Is that what you're doing? Are you kidnapping me?"

"Yes."

My heart skips a beat. I will admit my heart picks up speed as I remind myself this is Roman. I want him to beg me to love him. Maybe that makes me horrible, but considering the large...no...extraordinarily huge mistake he made by leaving me without a word, unprotected, he's lucky I'm even talking to him. Yes. I'm ignoring the note he left, but if he took a minute and thought about it, he would remember I never read his other messages. I told him I'd rather he read it to me in his sexy voice or simply that I didn't see it. Always some excuse or another.

"No." I fold my arms and glare at him.

"No? What do you mean, no?" He frowns.

Why do I want to laugh? This is a serious moment. A time to toe the line and let him know he's crossed it once again. He has to understand in the short period he's been away, I've found myself and a family. I still love him, but it's time for him to respect me.

I lean over the console and cup his cheek. "I love you, Roman, but it's time you let me go."

Chapter 24

Roman

A chill slides down my spine.

"I'm never letting you go." The words are out of my mouth without thought. Just as fast, I realize I mean them.

"Kidnapping me isn't the solution. I have a family now, and they'll be worried. For goodness sakes, my dad is your coach. You can't be serious."

"Kitty—"

"Katie. I'd rather you call me by my new name," she interrupts me in her sweet, but strangely hard voice.

I want to argue about her name choice, but it's not as important as the war going on between us. Then something she said slams into me.

"You love me?" My heart is about to beat out of my chest.

Her gaze drills into mine and then a tender smile lights her face. "So that finally sunk into your thick skull. Yeah. For quite a while now."

Unable to stop the need to touch her, I wrap her in my

arms, almost crawling over the console. "My soft, little kitten. You make me so happy. See. You must stay."

"No. I need to go back." She shoves me away and I back off.

"Please. Do not make this proud man beg." The twinkle in her eyes warns me I'll regret those words.

"It'll do you no good. I cried for several nights after you deserted me."

Without thought I grab her and pull her over the console into my lap.

"I never meant to hurt you. It wasn't my intention, *kotyonok*."

"I know that, but it hurt badly nevertheless."

Who is this woman I'm holding? Kitty never argued with me unless to tease. I'm not sure I like her new independence. I enjoy protecting her and having her needing me. Then again, my *khuy* hardens and lengthens when she disagrees with me. The best way for my agreeable pussycat to return is to show her what she's missing. In seconds, I lift her out of the car and sling her over my shoulder. She squeals and shouts at me to let her down. I continue into the house and up the stairs to our bedroom. The bed has been so empty without her warm, compact body cuddled to my own.

Blinded by my need to have her, I jerk down her pants, bringing her barely-there panties down to her ankles. It's when I reach to unbutton her blouse I realize she's not okay with what I'm doing. Tears spill from her eyes. Her cheeks redden from anger.

"I said no, Roman."

Shocked by her response, I step back. It's not like we haven't played this game before. But usually she's giggling by now.

She always loved how I took control and I would make sure she came twice to my every one. Fair, right?

I kneel on the floor near her, palms out. "I'm sorry, my Kitty. I see now you are not playing with me. My heart breaks from seeing you so unhappy." My hand rests on her knee, rubbing her soft skin to comfort her.

She slaps it away. "You make me so angry. You don't listen to me."

"I'm listening. I swear."

Her dark eyes narrow at me. "Why do you want to be with me?"

"Oh, baby, any man will be happy to be with you. You're fine with all your curves, girly ways, and the way your tongue—"

"That's not what I'm talking about it." She throws her head back and blinks. I hate seeing her upset.

"Why wouldn't I want you?"

I stand and begin to pace. From her expression, she's expecting more bullshit from me. Somehow I need for her to understand what I feel is real.

My frustration comes through each word that passes my lips. "When I'm with you, I work miracles. I do whatever I dream. Each time you smile, my world brightens. When I score a goal or get point or more in game, I can't wait to share with you. You understand me like no one ever has." I stop my pacing to check her acceptance of what I'm saying. I want her to see the truth in my eyes. "When I left, I thought only of me. I've regretted not telling you. Superstition interfered with my confidence in doing right by you." I cuss and say more, but the confusion on Kitty's face tells me I'm speaking in my native language. Returning to English, I softly say, "Deep inside I know you're my lucky charm."

"It's nice to know I'm equal to a rabbit's foot." She looks

away from me. She sits with her legs folded to the side, and in turn, hiding her beautiful pussy. Her blouse covers the other parts I so admire, but I don't think about that. If only her face will brighten again.

Damn. I'm a stupid man.

"You're more," I grunt out. The expectant look on her face tells me she's waiting for those three words women always crave. I can say it, can't I? But will I mean it? I'm not sure. But I need her. "You make me fucking-ly, stupidly happy. I care much for you."

As soon as the words are out of my mouth, I know it isn't enough. She deserves more. I can't give that to her yet. The room dims. My body becomes heavy with my decision.

She doesn't say anything for several seconds. She glares at me. Her lips straighten and then they slowly droop to sadness.

"Have I fucked up too badly?" I ask.

Does she have any idea that she's got my balls in her hands? For all I care, she can play with them all she wants. I'm so disgusted with myself.

Her head tilts as her gaze examines me. Whatever she's about to say will not make me happy.

"We're leaving in three days for Canada."

"What? No!" I squeeze my fingers into fists. The world tilts. I need her here with me.

"Turns out Dad knows a guy who knows a guy. And I should have a for-real passport soon." Her sad look clears. One of the many things I adore about her. She doesn't hold a grudge.

"I see." The desire to roar in fury rushes through my body, but I fight it. I don't want to frighten her. My shoulders slump. This is like losing in the seventh game of the finals in overtime.

She gives me a faint smile of sympathy. "Let me call Millie and tell her I'm okay, and I'll stay for one night. Then, you'll need to wait until I return for us to talk more. Millie's parents are actually vacationing at Lake Rosseau and the two families are getting together for the whole month. It's going to be amazing. Like a storybook family. I can't believe it's happening to me. It's great, isn't it?"

The excitement in her voice contradicts the frightened look on her face.

She's giving in to my need. The woman is compassionate. I can be just as merciful. So I work at wiping away her worries.

"They'll think you're fantastic, my kitten. Come. I'll help you call Millie." I reach in my pocket and pull out my cell phone. "I appreciate your offer to give me a second chance."

She looks at me, eyes wide. Why does she look so surprised by my words?

True, I want to find a way to make her stay. I'm still a selfish asshole. But I don't want her to resent being here. Papa will just have to understand, I must let her go to have any chance of her returning to me.

After giving me her usual tender smile, determination comes into her gaze. "Just understand. I return to the McMillans in the morning. This trip is important. Besides, I need time to think, you know, about us. So don't try to stop me from going."

Where is my sweet, biddable Kitty? I want to grip her shoulders and shake sense into her. Instead, I must show her what she's going to miss while tramping around Canada and making her decision on our future. Does my opinion matter? Do I get a chance to say how I feel?

I pull up the number and hit call. As soon as it starts to

ring, I hand the phone over to Kitty. While she's explaining to Millie, I quickly strip. Why take a chance of her changing her mind? To rush her along, I ease to my knees and begin to kiss her knees and slowly work up a smooth thigh. By the time I reach her pussy, she's breathless and says bye into the phone and drops it. I nuzzle her soft folds and lick her hard little clit. She moans and spreads her legs as her fingers dig into my scalp, allowing me access to what I miss so much. I feast on her until she explodes, her thighs tremble beneath my hands as I help her stand.

"Take your top off." Like the obedient girl I remember, she quickly sheds the silky material. "And your bra." The smooth satiny cups and straps drop away once she unfastens the back. I release a long breath. I haven't realize how much I yearned for the sight.

My hands move before I even think. Still on my knees, I lift and cup her beautiful tits, giving them a gentle squeeze.

"I missed you so much." I kiss her bellybutton, rimming it with my tongue, then I continue. "I missed this, holding you, touching you."

I don't know what I'm trying to say. Sure, we fucked in the locker room—a top ten fantasy come to life—but I haven't been able to immerse myself in what makes Kitty so different from other women. Her willingness to try anything, whenever, or wherever. Her kindness to everyone, including an asshole like me.

She threads her fingers into my hair.

"You broke my heart, but because of you, I found my father and a family who cares about me," she whispers.

She pushes me onto my back on the floor and slides a hand over my cock. I arch into her touch. She squeezes and releases as she strokes my hardness. Just as I'm about to beg, she leans down and licks me around the tip. I lift my hips as I thrust up into her mouth. She groans, vibrating every inch of me into her tight, hot throat. The woman could make a fortune giving head, but that talented mouth belongs to me and no one else.

"Baby, I'll never leave you again. Don't leave me." I hear the pleading in my voice. This is the first time in my life to beg a woman.

She sucks hard, and I release before I can pull out. She sits up and wipes her mouth with the back of her hand.

Fuck. That is so sexy. I feel my cock refilling with heat.

Without hesitation, she leans over and trails her tongue over my belly button and up my chest. I slide my hands into her hair and carefully pull her mouth to mine to kiss her. Her eyes half closed, she hums, the sound like a purr. I chuckle. How can she expect me to call her anything but Kitty?

I circle my arms around her waist and toss her onto the more comfortable bed. She squeals in pleasure. My hands grab her ankles and spread them wide to rub my semi-hard cock along her pussy. "That's what you do to me. I'm ready whenever you're around. In a few seconds, I will fuck you until you plead for me to let you rest from all the orgasms I give." Without needing to wait another second, I plunge in, and she moans.

"You feel wonderful." Her fingers dig into my hips. "Harder, faster."

"My pleasure, my sweet." Every counter thrust of her pelvis brings a delicious tightening in my balls. I want to slow down to make it last longer, but she's become a wild cat beneath me, and we fall over into the abyss of pleasure.

Throughout the night we sleep, make love, and sleep

some more. I dread when the sun comes up. Deep inside, I'm afraid she will go to Canada and never return.

Then I will be all alone.

Chapter 25

Kitty

The last three weeks have been wonderful. I met aunts, uncles, cousins, and so many sweet infants that I've been immersed in baby overload in the good way. Already we're planning next summer's trip and even had two cousins invite me over for the holidays in December. I have a feeling it will be a storybook Christmas this year, snow and all. I'm in heaven.

Standing on the back deck of my Uncle Liam's summer cabin—uncle! Actually, I have two uncles. I have another one who works for the NHL in Seattle—I admire the reflection of the moon on the lake a few yards away. The evening temperature is a little cooler than I'm used to, but I find it invigorating. With a long inhale, I take in the scent of pine. I'm not sure the sigh I release is from how tired I am—I actually learned the basics to kayaking today—or from missing Roman so much.

From his posts on Instagram that the teenagers have shown me, his training is at full speed ahead. His athletic trainer has him doing all types of exercises he'd never tried before. They are to help him pick up speed and strengthen his balance. I saw the short video of where he hops onto air-filled rings, one foot at a time, challenging his balance. From the comments he makes, he swears he feels stronger and steadier than ever.

"What are you doing out here all alone?"

Dad places an arm around my shoulder and squeezes me to his side. Then he leans on the rail with his elbows. I still have to pinch myself whenever I look up and see him smiling with such pride at me. Usually, he does that when one of my cousins quizzes me on hockey. I've been proclaimed a true Canadian at heart since I answered all of the questions correctly. The clincher was when I proclaimed Wayne Gretzky as the best of the best and then argued the styles of goalies Rinne and Fleury. They knew I loved the game as much as any Canadian.

Everyone welcomed me with open arms, and no one referred to me as a puck bunny or ignored my opinion. I feel like I belong. I've found my people.

"I'm just enjoying the view." The lake glistens in the moonlight.

"You look sad."

"A little. I miss Roman. I haven't heard from him since I left. He has my number. Thank you again for my cell phone by the way." Has he given up on me? "Do you know if he's seeing someone else?" He's private and mainly talks about hockey and the causes he personally cares about and the ones the team supports. Other people like to spread rumors of the more intimate kind. Up until now, I struggled not to ask my dad about him. It's unfair to have Roman's coach check on his personal life. "Pretend I didn't ask that. I don't want you spying on your players."

Dad grunts as if saying he agrees.

After a few more seconds, he looks my way. "If you love

him that much, maybe you need to give him a second chance."

"Second chance? I did. I forgave him for leaving me without a word and for the blonde."

"Are you sure?" He rests a hip against the railing and faces me. "I think deep inside you're still angry with him. You hoped he'd miss you as much as you miss him. Maybe with you not even attempting to call is a little revenge tagged onto it."

"Well, if I thought that, it backfired. Not a word and from what little I see on the Internet he doesn't act like he's missing me." To be fair, he's mostly doing promo stuff for the team's and his charities.

"I don't know what you're looking for from him, but I do know he's an ambitious player. He works hard to improve his game and has always acted aboveboard when it comes to his attitude toward women. From what I've seen, anyway. Maybe you need to give the fellow a break."

"You're probably right." That is, if he still wants another chance. He may have moved on. "We're going back home next week, right?"

He nods.

"I'll find out then if he's wants to be with me."

"Are you sure you want to wait that long?"

"Yes. If he's the one, he'll still be waiting for me."

"That's my girl. Stand by your decision even if it makes you miserable."

I give him some side-eye. Is he teasing me? I raise my eyebrows

He reaches over and hugs me with one arm. "Sometimes we have to give in, if we really want something or someone. If he's the kind of man I think he is, he will. Then again, do you think I would've waited on the bench long for Millie to decide?"

"You know, you're confusing me." I shake my head. "When we first arrived, you said to wait as the heart will grow fonder. Now you tell me I'll lose my man if I'm not around. You really need to make up your mind." I flash him a grin to show I'm teasing back. A little.

"You misunderstood. I'm saying if he's in love with you, he'll never give you time to find someone else. You've had plenty of opportunities. Liam's guys would love to date you." Dad is talking about the AHL team my uncle coaches in upstate New York. Several of them have dropped by. A few are my age, but I feel decades older.

"But I'm not the same girl I was over a month ago. I can't go back to being the person who waits for the guy to tire of her before moving on to the next one." I see Dad flinch. He hates knowing what I did to survive. Really, I need to remember he loves and cares for me. "I want a family. I want permanence. I want a man to love me and only me in the way you and Millie love each other."

I look up and I notice the moonlight on his face. Tears fill his eyes.

"Oh, sweetheart, you deserve that and more." He pulls me against his chest and tightens his hold. My nose squashes against his chest. I don't care. For so many years I dreamed of this, having a dad to confide in and help me understand men and the world.

I wiggle to breathe.

He chuckles and releases me. "Sorry about that. I get carried away. You can ask Millie and the kids about that."

I laugh with him. Hannah and the guys have told me how he's the mushy one as he feels guilty for leaving them and their mom alone so much because of his job. Not that he's a pushover when it comes to school and dating.

"Hey, Katie, Uncle Liam said he has someone he wants to introduce you to." Millie stands at the sliding glass door with a mischievous look on her face.

"He better be older than eighteen. It gets a little creepy being ogled by a teenager," I say, teasing her about the last skater he'd introduced me to. Sure, he had a beard and did look to be twenty-one at least. They do grow them bigger in Canada.

As soon as I walk in the door, I know something is wrong. It's too quiet.

"Hello, Kitty...uh...Katie."

My breath leaves my lungs. I had forgotten how handsome he is. Well, the way I think of handsome. Professional hockey player handsome. The bump on the bridge of his nose from being broken so many times, the scar near his upper lip, the chipped front tooth on top, the three-day beard, and his black eye. That last one is new. Probably a mishap during training. He'd told me before he plans to fix his tooth and nose when he retires. He claims it's just a waste of time and money while he's playing. Beyond all of that, his broad shoulders and chest, muscled arms, small hips, and bulging thighs filling out faded jeans are enough to make any woman sigh.

Eyes dark blue like a deep sea stare back at me. What is he doing here? How does he know Uncle Liam? Is this a joke?

"Why don't we leave these two alone for a little while?" Uncle Liam waves everyone out of his living room, grabbing Dad's arm and whispering to him when he refuses to budge. They finally leave.

"How do you know Uncle Liam?" I look down and

notice I'm bunching up my blouse in two fists. I let it go and look back up at Roman.

"I came up a couple years ago and helped with a summer program before returning when camp started."

"It's nice for you to come by and visit with him."

"I didn't come to see him. He understands why I'm here."

I wait a few seconds to see what he'll say, but he remains quiet. His gaze searches my face. Have I changed?

"Well, why are you here?" I swear my nervousness causes me to be rude. "Sorry. Would you like a drink? We have tea, coffee, beer, and some type of wine Millie swears was made by the angels. Still tastes horrible to me." I press a finger to my lips. "Don't tell her I said that."

One corner of his mouth lifts. "I promise."

His accent comes through on the last word. Russian is a sexy accent. Of course, I'm biased as I'm still in love with him.

A few more seconds go by. Now he's making me nervous again.

"Roman..."

"Kitty..."

We say it simultaneously.

I smile and then sigh. "Are we going to stand here all night? How about sitting down?"

"I'm so sorry, my sweet little *kiska*."

I jerk back my head as my eyebrows furrow. "Sorry? Sorry for what?"

He swipes his hands down those nice jeans. "For everything. For treating you the way I did. For not talking to you. For allowing myself to get in that regretful position with the blonde. For letting you leave. I've been a robot for the last three weeks. Doing what my new agent tells me, what's expected of me, but I've been frozen inside. I know if I think hard on the last couple months and all the wrong decisions I've made, I'll go crazy. Hell, I think I have gone off the deep end long before I fucked up and left you alone for my own selfish reasons."

I remain standing, trying to wrap my mind around everything he said. He looks and sounds earnest. Being upfront with myself, I have to admit he's never lied to me. The worst he's done is not to tell me the whole truth. His biggest sin is not trusting me. I believe he understands that now.

"Where do we go from here?" I ask.

"Marry me. I need you to be mine and only mine."

"And you? Who will you belong to?" This is when I expect him to tell me how his first concern is his job, his first love, hockey.

"You."

Well, that's unexpected.

Chapter 26

Roman

Who will you belong to?

I answer with the honest truth. "You."

Kitty doesn't immediately respond. Her dark eyes stare at me as if I lost my mind, and I'm ignorant about the basic things of life.

"Do you not believe me?" I ask her.

"In the months I've known you, you talked only about hockey being your first love, your mistress, your everything." She tilts her head and gently smiles.

Damn, I miss her so fucking much. Every little emotion she betrays on her face is so dear to me. She speaks the truth. What she does not know is that I'm obsessed with her.

"Don't you understand what you mean to me? I knew," I thump my chest, "you special on first day I met you. You sat in booth crying, not to hide in shame or look around for sympathy. When I flirted with you, you gave same smile. I knew I needed take care of you." I struggle to think fast enough of the English words I need to say. "We happy. Then I fuck up." I cup her cheek and sweep my thumb over her smooth skin. Taking a deep breath regaining a little of my senses, I step away from her. "You had plenty time to think, but think more tonight and tomorrow. Come to me. I stay at the Rosseau Muskoka Resort." I give her a small envelope with a number written on the outside and a card-key inside. "I'll be there from eight to midnight, if you still want me. If you do not show up, I will understand."

My heart fills my throat. I'm taking a big chance. She may not want me any longer. That will be a first. As it is the first time for me to love someone besides family, I'm afraid she may not love me enough in turn. She has no idea I will do anything for her.

I leave after gently kissing her goodnight. It takes all of my self-control not to strip her there in her uncle's home with family nearby. I must confess I care little if her father— my head coach—caught me. She belongs to me, she's my heart.

The next morning I speak with my agent. I'm told a Canadian team and a U.S. West Coast team are asking about me. If the offer from the Edge is not what I want, I become an unrestricted, free agent by July. The deal so far from my current team isn't at the level I expect after my success last season and in Russia. There is time to jack up the price during the negotiations. Preseason doesn't start until September.

I exercise in the hotel's fitness center for about two hours in the hope of working off some energy. The day drags by. I check out a few activities, but what if she decides to come over early, and I'm not here? So I go to the bar and drink a soda—I need to have my wits about me—and watch a commentator show the top thirty defensemen. My spirits begin to dip as I show up at number seventeen. Fuck. I tell myself I should be happy I'm on the list and not at the bottom. Fuck. I ask the bartender to add whiskey to my half-filled glass.

By seven-thirty, I'm punching the button in the elevator for my floor. I need time to brush my teeth and check my appearance. The light in the room comes from the open curtains. Love summertime and long daylight hours.

When eight o'clock arrives, the silence begins to bother me. I click on the TV and change the channel to a lacrosse game. After turning down the volume, I pace through the living area of the suite. The clock shows nine, and I sit in a hard, straight-back chair. I'm afraid if I recline on the sofa, I'll doze off. I want to be fully awake when she walks in.

The next hour plods along. A darkness settles around me, matching the dimness in the room as the sun sinks into the horizon. Kitty has obviously decided to stay with her family. How can I deny her what she's dreamed about all her life? I can offer the same, but I know she views me as a gamble.

I lean forward, elbows on my knees, and bury my face into my hands. How long before I do something stupid like go and demand to see her? My cell phone's alarm buzzes. I ignore it as it continues to vibrate. It's midnight. Still no Kitty.

Disgusted with myself, I push off the chair. My emotions freeze from the blow. I refuse to cry. I come from a strong line of manly-men. We do not cry over women. Then I remember my dad crying like a baby when my mother died. That's understandable. Thankfully, Kitty is alive and well.

For now, I need to prepare to leave tomorrow. After stripping down, I stride into the bathroom and turn on the shower. Without waiting for the water to warm, I step into the stall and begin washing up. The cold water yanks me out of my numbness.

I imagine my kitten moving on to another man and the thought rips through my guts. At first, I think I'm shaking because of the icy water, but it has warmed considerably. I realize I'm crying. Pressing my palms flat on the wall, I take a deep breath and shake my head until I regain control.

Time to stop thinking of the only woman to break my heart. Maybe after I arrive at home, I can let myself indulge in self-pity.

I step out and dry off, rubbing the towel over my hair before wrapping it around my hips. When I open the door into the room, I swear I smell her subtle scent of perfume, and the mango scented shampoo she loves. No one in the bedroom or living area. With a glance at the clock on the desk, I see it's almost one in the morning. She's probably sound asleep at her uncle's vacation cabin.

Combing my damp hair with my fingers, I sit on the edge of the bed and look at my cell phone with a yearning that hurts. No calls or texts. I thumb the recent list and almost touch her number. No. I do have some pride. That's why I haven't called before. No need to start now.

I toss my phone onto the nightstand and rise to my feet to whip off the towel.

"Now that's something to behold."

Turning quickly, I knock the lamp onto the floor. "What the fuck—"

I swallow the rest of the words. Kitty leans her shoulder against the door frame leading into the bedroom. A glint of mischief twinkles in her eyes.

I pick up the lamp and place it back on the nightstand.

"Sorry to scare you. I did use the key. You were taking a

shower, and I decided to step out onto the balcony and enjoy the nice evening."

A greenish-blue summer dress clings to her shapely body. The matching sweater gives her a virginal look. I'm glad it's so early in the morning. There are rarely any people in the lobby or in the elevators. This view belongs to me.

I stride up to her and stop, only an inch away. She tilts her head back and looks into my eyes. Her beloved face is missing its usual smile.

"You're here," I say the obvious.

The corners of her mouth lift. Finally.

"Yeah. I'm not a mirage. Sorry I was late."

I cup her cheeks, my thumbs caress those expressive corners.

"I love you," I whisper. "I want you to be part of every moment of my life. You are my heart." Tears well up in her eyes, and I kiss her forehead as my thumb drifts across her soft lips. "No, no, no. Did I say it wrong? It's a good thing, I promise."

"You said it perfectly while standing there without a stitch on." She smirks. "You must always tell me that whenever you're naked. It's a good thing you said you loved me. It would be most awkward if you didn't say it after I told my dad I knew deep inside that you loved me. Then I might have to ask him to kick your fine ass." She winks and then her tongue shoots out to lick my thumb.

My dick thickens so fast my head becomes light.

"Yes. It's a good thing. I don't want daughter to hate me if I pound her father into the ground."

"No kicking or pounding. Well, not the type that hurts." Her wicked grin has me nearly coming where I stand. She knows all the buttons to push until I'm crazy with lust.

"Ah, my naughty little kitten. One of the many things I

love about you." I take her mouth and show her how happy I am. My tongue strokes hers. My hands clasp her body against mine. I lift her up to move my lips to her neck. Skin so silky I nip at her shoulder. A gasp, part surprise and part need, fills the room. I pull her simple dress and sweater over her head and then hold her away.

The thin material of her bra reveals the large areola and hard nipple in the center of each breast. I nip at the hard nub. She gasps again. We've had sex many times, but this time everything feels different. It's more.

I unclasp the back and her bra falls away. Cupping their fullness, I lift them to my mouth, licking and sucking the tips as her breathing becomes heavy and loud.

Her fingers dip into my hips as she tugs me closer. I inhale as her cool hand grips my length. I exhale and lean my head back, closing my eyes in the ecstasy of her delicate hand clasping me again.

She starts to sink to her knees, but I stop her.

"No. Not this time." I love her blow jobs, but I plan to show her how much she means to me. With a light shove, she lands on the bed, her toes touching the carpeted floor. I slip off her shoes. The final piece of material between us has to go. I hook my fingers over the sides and peel the tiny, lacy panties down her smooth legs. The sweet, musky scent of a woman's pussy ready for her lover is better than any drug sold on the black market. Kitty's is doubly so. "You better grip the sheets and hold on."

I dip my tongue and part her folds. Damn, I love the taste of her. I suckle on her clit, and she releases a long moan as her thighs tighten around my head. A nudge with my shoulders opens her legs wider and then I pull her butt closer to the edge. As I lick and suck, my hands glide up to cover her tits. I massage their fullness, occasionally pinching and tugging the tips. She arches and thrusts her hips, silently begging for more.

When I feel her body begin to stiffen, I stand, stroking my cock as I look at her. She lifts her head to see what I'm doing. She bites one side of her bottom lip. Her gaze remains on me. The head of my cock skims her glistening opening.

"Now, I fuck you good."

With a hard plunge into her hot pussy, I hear her cry out in pleasure, and I begin to piston into her. My thumb rests on her clit and presses hard. I rub in a circle, again and again. Nothing gentle with my touch. Her body bows as she orgasms. I want to hold off and enjoy the way her pussy clamps and releases me over and over again, but my greedy cock lets go and I give a long exhale. All of my strength is gone. So not to hurt my kitten, I fall to the side and pull her into my arms.

"You never said yes."

"Yes?"

Is she teasing me?

I rest my head into a palm and look down at her. Her eyes shine with humor.

"I want to marry you. You have not agreed," I grumble.

"No, I haven't."

"What? You love me. I love you. You do not want to marry?"

"True, but lots of people love each other and do not need a piece of paper, do not need to make it legal."

I want to pull my hair out. This woman is driving me crazy.

"You will belong to me and everyone will know. How can I convince you that we need to do this thing?"

"Maybe you need to figure that out. If this is what you want, you'll need to show me."

Leaning over, I kiss her. I possess her. She is mine. My teeth nip at her bottom lip and then I glide my tongue across it.

I cup and lift one breast as I press a kiss to the underside of the full mound. The tip is bead hard against my palm. She moans and her body arches with hunger.

She grabs my hand and pushes it away.

"No. This is not what I mean. I need more from you. Not sex, though it's lovely indeed, and I don't mean anything you can buy."

All of the air releases from my body. How did she know I'm trying to imagine the perfect gift? Of course, an engagement ring to be proud of, but more. Cars, homes, fancy clothes, anything that will make her happy.

"What must I do to coax you into marrying me?"

"If you want me to marry you that badly, you'll think of the proper way to ask me again."

Proper?

I pull her into my arms, her back to my chest. I want this woman in my bed forever. I want everyone to know she belongs to me.

Hmm, I believe I have the perfect idea.

Chapter 27

Kitty

Since our return from Canada, the last few weeks have been insane. Between Roman's different promo and charity obligations, we are able to have a normal dating life. He didn't like that I refused to move back in with him, but at the same time he understood. I wanted more time with my family, and he still hasn't thought of the proper way to propose.

"Where are you and Roman going tonight?" Hannah hesitates in the doorway of my bedroom.

I wave her in. She's the best little sister I could've ever dreamed of. I don't know if I stood in her shoes if I'd like to share my mom and dad with a stranger.

"A friend of a friend of his is opening a restaurant and invited us for the trial run. So lots of food to check out. Should be fun. Several of his teammates will be there."

"Will Mark Jones be there?" Hannah runs her finger over the pretty shade of the lamp sitting on the night stand.

Mark is the newest winger for the Edge and only nineteen years old. Still too old for Hannah. Besides, her father will make Mark's life a misery if he even looks her way. I can't blame her for the interest, the guy is good-looking and a charmer. Maybe too charming for his own good.

"I believe I heard his and his girlfriend's names were mentioned." I tell myself it's best to keep her feet planted on earth.

A shadow crosses her face for a moment, but then she brightens. "I start practice in two weeks for next season. Dad said he'll take me to the rink this weekend and work with me on my slap shots."

I've learned recently Dad had been known for his slap shots during his playing days. The two older boys were getting a reputation for having powerful shots too. Obviously, he's taught them as he'll teach his daughter.

Sure, it appears I believe the McMillans are awesome people and near to perfect. Well, yeah, but like all families, they do have their faults. Really, but they are so small. Such as Dad snores. Micah never picks up his stinky socks and leaves them everywhere. Millie is a fiend when it comes to being on schedule and everybody has to abide. And Hannah, well, Hannah and Sam are perfect or their faults are mine and don't bother me.

Hannah sits on my bed and watches as I finish my makeup. She doesn't care about makeup yet, but is great at judging if I have everything even. I stand and slip on my heels. Roman said the affair is dressy. So I'm wearing a simple cocktail length black dress with silver trim around the neck. My necklace has a single diamond drop, the same as my earrings. Presents from Roman.

"Katie, Roman's here." Millie walks in. "Oh, you look so pretty. You'll make Roman nuts trying to keep the other men from checking you out." She presses her cheek to mine and smiles at me from the mirror. "You better hurry, Guy has him cornered."

I pick up my purse and head into the hallway after kissing Hannah's and then Millie's cheeks. Dad has been pushing Roman to hurry up and propose. I asked Dad to not worry, Roman will figure out the best way. So far, Roman acts like he hasn't changed his mind, but why is it taking forever?

My gaze goes straight to where the two men who mean everything in my life stood. Dad and Roman are in the far corner, talking nearly nose-to-nose. They're close to the same height, but Dad outweighs Roman by twenty pounds. With Roman's constant training and Dad's inclination for Millie's homemade cheese cake, it's no surprise.

As I walk up to the men, they fall silent. I'm not too sure I like this. They better be playing nice.

"I hope you two are not arguing." I take in their sheepish expressions and shake my head. "Whatever you two are up to, make sure I'm not involved." I ignore their smirks. Men. My gaze settles on Roman. "I'm ready, if you are?"

"Let's go."

From what Roman has told me since settling into his car, the restaurant is only fifteen minutes away, but twenty minutes have gone by and he's driving along a street with an awesome view of the city.

"Aren't we going a little out of our way?"

Roman glances over to me before returning his attention to the road. "I thought it best to miss a little of the crowd. Make an entrance." He does love the attention, and I understand it's all part of his reputation in being a showman along with a great hockey player.

Another five minutes slip by, and we pull up to a valet stand in front of a small, white building in the Art Deco style. With discreet landscape lights shining on the bright flowers and well-maintained shrubbery along the curving sidewalk to the door, the aromas and colors are a special treat to the senses.

A chill eases down my spine as I stand outside the restaurant. The leaves ruffling in the trees and traffic passing by makes it appear deserted. No one is waiting outside, and no music is playing. Are we at the wrong place? Not a good sign for the dress rehearsal of the grand opening in two days.

"Are you sure we have the right night?" I ask with concern in my voice.

Roman rests his arm over my shoulders. "Don't worry. They're inside." He opens the door, and where a maître d' normally stands, the outer chamber is empty. In fact, the whole dining area is dark. Again, I get a creepy feeling.

"What's going on? Did we go to the wrong restaurant?" I turn to Roman to see him going down on one knee. In his hand is a black velvet box. I never imagined he would do something so cliché, but I'm overwhelmed by the sweetness of it. Just what I want. Something perfectly normal.

"My Kitty, my Katie Summerville—I call you whatever you want." His voice deepens. "I have found in you my soul-mate, my best friend, my woman." A few chuckles bounce around the room though I can't see anyone, but my attention remains on Roman's dear face. "I cannot live without you. I'm less of a man without you near. Will you do me, a lowly grinder, the honor of accepting my heart and my ring? Be my wife. Please. I love you—forever—my sweet *kiska.*"

Despite his sexy accent becoming heavier as he spoke, I can tell he practiced. My heart pounds, thinking of Roman working on the speech, carefully choosing each word. He's more of a seat-of-his-pants sort of man. He worked hard on this just for me.

My hands fly to my cheeks. I never imagined Roman being so romantic. I look at his hand, holding out the box. It's shaking. My sexy Russian is nervous. A man who can face without fear five men who are trying to slam him against board, glass, and ice is afraid of my answer.

"Yes. Of course, I'll marry you."

Before I can say he's much more than a grinder, the lights come on and an excited cry of around a hundred people shout out their joy. I jump and take in everyone standing in the dining room, smiling and clapping. At least, that explains the chuckles I heard.

"You planned this," I say in more of a statement than question. My cheeks are a little heated from embarrassment but also with unrestrained happiness.

"I wanted witnesses if you said yes. Then you can't back out."

Unable to hold it, I laugh louder than I have in a long time. His eyes widen in surprise and then his arms come around me. His kiss is gentle and I want more, but with all the shouts of congratulations and comments, I know we can wait.

He leads me into the dining room where people surround us, clapping his back and hugging me. When we stop in front of a tall, gray-haired, stern-looking man, I smile. The grin that slowly grows on his face is so familiar. I remember him now from the restaurant. Roman's dad, Sergei. From the times I spoke to him over the phone, I know he's a blunt man with a dry wit. Silly as it may be, I'm a little scared of him. I'm aware of how much his opinion matters to Roman and I want him to like me.

Without saying a word to his son, he pulls me out of Roman's hold and then wraps his strong arms around me and squeezes. I squeak.

"You are what my son needs. A good woman with a warm heart and knows how to keep his bed hot between the sheets."

"Papa! No need to embarrass your future daughter-in-law."

A man with the similar looks of Roman, but slightly shorter, walks up to stand next to Sergei. "Hello, Kitty. I'm Erik, the older brother to this troublemaker." He grabs Roman by the shoulders and pulls him in for a bear hug.

"Where is Kristina?" Roman asks.

"Here I am." She rubs her stomach and smiles at me. "I'm this brute's wife." She shoves Erik and laughs.

"So nice to finally meet you and Erik." I left it hanging as if Roman spoke of him often. He mentioned his brother only one time and never the wife. From what little I sensed at the time, his father prefers Erik because of his career choice. From the way Sergei is talking with and looking at Roman, I believe he's feeling more paternal toward his youngest. Maybe he worries about his son because his career is one hundred times more dangerous than the eldest's.

My family—such beautiful words—join the crowd around me. The kisses and hugs make me feel more loved than a person can possibly handle, but I do my best. For I feel like I'm not totally outnumbered by family and friends of the man I'm with.

Dad leans down and looks into my eyes. "Are you sure this is what you want?"

"Yes. More than I ever imagined. I know now he loves me as much as I do him."

He raises his eyebrows. "All right then. I guess I better not bench him, heh?"

"Not unless it's best for the team," I tease.

"That's my girl." He kisses me on the top of my head and chuckles. The rest of the McMillan crew comes in to tease and hug me. I love these wonderful people.

The owner of the restaurant taps on a glass to instruct everyone to take a flute of champagne or sparkling grape juice from the waitstaff. We raise our glasses and the whole restaurant congratulates us. Once everyone is seated, they start taking orders. The rest of the evening is like a lovely dream. Excellent food and loving company.

As we're testing a few desserts, Roman turns to me. "Come home with me tonight. Stay."

I lightly kiss his lips, but pull back before he can make it more. His face begins to fall, certain I'm about to say no.

"Okay." Unable to resist, my fingers glide over his cheek to his strong neck.

He lifts my hand and kisses each tip.

We leave without a word. Everyone appears to know we are in love and need our time alone.

Perfect.

Chapter 28

Kitty's & Roman's Epilogues

Kitty's Epilogue

Hard to believe in two days I will be marrying the love of my life. Dad and I tried talking Roman into waiting until next summer. Then there would be enough time to do everything our families plan, including a honeymoon to Russia. But he refuses to listen.

So here I am going on a girls' night out with a handful of the other players' wives and girlfriends. They call it a bachelorette party, but it's nothing more than hitting a few nightclubs before the limo takes us back to our homes. That's okay. I appreciate the gesture considering they barely know me.

At the same time, the men are partying at a local strip club. I told Roman it's best to enjoy it now as I intend to go with him from now on. As he thought I was about to tell him he'll never go again, he roars with laughter and says I'll be the best wife ever.

We started at the Sanctuary, went on to the Havana Club, and then landed at the Tongue and Groove. Though it might be odd to most of the women with me, I rarely visited nightclubs. Most of the bars I know were from the ones past boyfriends visited or owned. I'm amazed by how many restaurants and bars are owned by sport figures.

Sitting at the table reserved for the party, I watch as Jennifer and Ashley dance together. Several men linger in a circle to watch their antics. The women are shaking and rubbing against each other. I hear the close friends are dating two forwards who are nearly inseparable. I can only imagine what goes on in private between the couples.

The woman sitting next to me, Emily, has two children. Millie is babysitting so Emily can go out. I have to say I like her best. She's excited to be "an adult" for the night. Her husband is a center and will probably retire after this year. From what I hear, he's planning to return to a local university and finish the law degree he started before being signed up originally by Detroit, and later moving from one team to another until he landed with the Edge. Unlike what a lot of people believe, just because you play for the NHL, it doesn't mean you're set financially for life. Many of the skaters don't manage their money well, or they remain on the fourth line. Sometimes they are sent down to the affiliate team, making a much smaller scale than the stars of the teams.

The last two of our party, Heather and Jessica, are chatting with some friends who walked over to say hi. We were introduced to the friends, but I couldn't hear their names over the loud music. I sure do feel old.

"Hey, Jessica and I have been invited to meet Charles Barkley. I love his sense of humor. He's hanging with some friends of mine. We'll be back by the time the limo shows up. Maybe." They giggle and, without waiting for a reply, the two women turn and wind their way through the crowd. I see the big guy at a table filled with beautiful women and a few tall, built men, probably members of the Atlanta Hawks.

"More champagne for us," Emily says, lifting her glass to clink against mine.

I smile and sip. Although not a big drinker, after Millie persuaded me to try it, I've decided I do like a glass on occasion. For the next fifteen minutes, we sit and people watch. She points out a couple of actors who are said to be making a film nearby.

"Sorry, but I need to go to the ladies room. Want to go with me? I'm hoping the line isn't long." Emily and I decide whoever designs nightclubs forget women need more time to take care of business, thus need more stalls and mirrors.

"I'll stay here and keep an eye on our drinks so we won't have to reorder." Too dangerous to leave our drinks with psychos sneaking date rape drugs in them at the first chance.

"Oh, that's right. Smart thinking. It's been so long since I've gone anywhere without the kids. Love them, but I needed this." She laughs. "Thanks. I'll be back as soon as I can." She slowly makes her way down to the main floor and then around to a small hallway.

It feels funny sitting alone in the reserved area. A few people look hard at me, probably trying to guess if I'm a celebrity or someone they should know.

I ignore them and continue to people watch. The music's beat thrums from my feet up my body. I begin to sway to the music. Though I'm alone, I'm happy. Today, I've made a new friend. Emily is kind and laid back. I have a family with a Dad and siblings and a great stepmother. I'm about to marry the man I love. He loves me. So very happy.

"Well, I heard you got Roman wrapped around your little pinkie after all."

Cringing, I recognize that voice. I carefully turn to face Casey Perry, Roman's former agent. The one who lied and tried his best to get in my pants. The asshole.

Though I have hundreds of people surrounding me, I don't trust Casey not to try something, especially upon seeing the hatred shining out of his beady eyes.

"Casey." My shoulders refuse to relax. I don't want him to know how afraid I am of him. From the smirk crossing his face, I didn't succeed. I have no idea why he hates me and probably will never know.

"Where's your limp-dick boyfriend?"

The man really thinks he has nothing to fear of Roman.

"I think it's best if you move on," I warn.

He reaches over the table and touches my hair. "If you want to try a real man, you only need to come with me. I'll show you my big dick," he says in a tone he thinks is sexy.

Instead, it creeps me out. Despite his obvious hate for me, he still thinks he's so charming.

I spread my palm over his face and push. He stumbles back. He didn't expect that. Truthfully, my actions surprise me too.

Raising his open hand, he prepares to backhand me. I gasp when Roman appears from nowhere and grabs his wrist.

"If you laid a hand on her, you regret it." Roman's slightly shorter than the former self-proclaimed basketball star, but Casey's face pales as Roman glares at the man. "You have the guts to hit me. Or women only you like to terrorize?" Roman shouts a string of Russian words that are likely not very nice.

"You won't dare hit me? I will ensure you never play again."

"No. Not here." Roman nods over his left shoulder.

"There are two men behind me, their job is to take out trash. But we can meet at O'Reilly's Gym. They have ring I can pound you in ground, legally. Or you too chicken-shit?"

"You're crazy." Casey jerks his hand away from Roman's hold. "You deserve the slut."

I jump between the men and press my whole body against Roman's. He trembles from head to toe in pure anger.

"He's not worth it. Let him destroy his own business." I encircle his neck and pull him down to whisper in his ear. "Once the word is out what he did and how he's a coward—you know he won't show up at the gym—his career will be over. No one will ever trust him."

He drags his gaze from Casey's to mine. The tension in his face and shoulders eases.

"You're right." Then he turns his attention back to Casey. "I'll be at the gym tomorrow at 8 a.m. You be there."

"I have commitments."

"Then you don't show and prove everyone you are base coward." Roman places his arm around my shoulder and leads me away. "Limo is here. Time for us to go home. Good?"

I love his care for me. I love this man so much.

"Yes. Good. Very good."

Roman's Epilogue

The wedding that was to be only twenty, thirty people at most, turned into over a hundred. Kitty was so scared and worried too much. But all went well. At least, that is what I say. She tells me differently.

The most important thing is she's in my bed and in my

arms and will no longer disappear. I have to leave at the butt-crack of dawn—love my new American expression—but so worth knowing she belongs to me.

She lifts her head from my shoulder and leans over. Her delicate fingers caress my temple.

"What are you smiling about?" Her grin is as big as mine.

"I'm thinking about getting up at the butt-crack of dawn."

"I could shoot Sam for using that phrase around you. Don't be saying it in any of your interviews. It's not proper. You want to stay out of trouble." She kisses my cheek.

Warmth wells up in my chest. She makes me so happy. No one has cared for me as much as she does.

"I know what to say. The other day when the reporter showed up at the gym, I didn't call Casey a candy-ass bastard for not showing up." Actually, I insinuated that he was having problems keeping clients. I only guessed, but it turns out to be true.

He not only lost his NHL clients but half of his NBA ones. More information came out the day after the confrontation that he'd sexually harassed a couple of other clients' girlfriends.

The man is in deep shit. Not my problem anymore.

I scoop up my kitten and kiss her long and deeply. When I let us both breathe, she caresses my cheek.

"I will miss you while you're in L.A. and San Jose."

"You will be here when I return?"

"Yes. Millie and I are taking Hannah to buy her a Halloween costume. She doesn't want to wait until they are picked over. It appears one of the boys at her school has already asked her out to a party."

"And McMillan is allowing her to go?"

"Of course. Hannah and the boy will meet at the party. Millie has already confirmed the parents will be at the house along with a few other adults. So all safe."

"Our daughter will not go to boy-girl party until she is out of college."

She rolls her eyes and laughs.

"You are crazy. We don't have to worry about that for a long time." She shakes her finger at me.

I look down at her stomach.

"When can we get you pregnant?"

"What? We haven't been married twenty-four hours. Give it time. We'll talk about it next year. I want a little more time with you before I have to share."

I kiss her again. She is so adorable.

She laughs and I laugh with her.

I raise my head, glaring at the spot where a fist is banging and shaking the wall. "Quit that, old man! Your room is on the other side of the house. We are not disturbing you." I shake my head. "We should have gone to hotel."

"It's okay." Her delicate hand cups the side of my face. "We have many more nights to be together and no one will bother us. I think it's cute. He worries you won't be rested for the opening game."

"My papa and Erik like you."

"I had a feeling, considering how many times they hugged me. My ribs are sore."

Without asking, I pull back and look at her sexy body. I had insisted on the lights being on, and she said okay to the one in the bathroom. It shone across the mattress. She giggles as I feel up and down her ribs and move her side to side, looking for bruises.

"I see nothing. Where do they hurt? I'll knock my family into next week for this."

She wraps her arms below her tits. My attention is quickly drawn to the beautiful mounds of femininity. I had no idea that I was such a tit man. My usual favorite part of a woman's body was her ass. She was sitting down when I met her and I noticed her nice tits. But I have to say I'm a lucky man. Her ass is prime A.

"No. Leave your family alone. They are fine. They weren't the only ones squeezing me tight, and no, nothing to worry about. All were gentlemen."

Relief has me dropping onto my back and pulling her on top of me.

"Good. We would have a hard time with so many being on the IR list." Normally, only two or three people are on the injury reserve list and a couple on the healthy scratch.

She pushes up, her hands on my shoulders, and her hips align with mine. My cock begins to lengthen and harden again.

"I was thinking. You will be gone for four days. One full day without practice or a game. What if I fly out and meet you in L.A.?"

Surprised does not cover my feelings.

"You will do this for me?" I miss her so much when I'm on the road. My Russia trip being the worst. Why I had not thought ahead? I have no idea. Maybe because I was an idiot. No more.

"Yes. Millie is going and wants me to go too. I figure this is a good time for me to experience air travel that far." The softness on her face tells me how much she wants to do this for me.

"That sounds good. Very good. I will text Millie my room number."

"You can text it to me. I'm really good with numbers. Just keep any English words you type simple for now."

I'm so proud of my kitten. So much she's been through, and still she's sweet, brave, and so lovable. She claims once she masters reading and writing American English, she will tackle Russian. As I said, brave girl.

My lips lightly touch hers. "I love you, my *kiska*."

"*Ya tebya lyublyu*," she says, blushing.

Ah, my girl loves me too.

About the Author

CARLA SWAFFORD loves romance novels, action/adventure movies, and men, and her books reflect that. And on top of it all, she's crazy about hockey, and thankfully, no one has made her turn in her Southern Belle card.

So, it's no surprise she writes spicy romantic suspense filled with mercenaries, motorcycle one-percenters, and southern criminals. And in the last few years, she's included sexy hockey players in books without suspense, except for the kind that asks, how will they ever find their happily ever after?

Married to her high school sweetheart, she lives in the Southeast U.S. To find out more about Carla, visit her Facebook, Instagram, and TikTok pages. Be sure to join her newsletter.

Website: carlaswafford.com

Other Books by Carla Swafford

THE CIRCLE SERIES

Circle of Desire

Circle of Danger

Circle of Deception

Circle of Dishonor (novella)

Circle of Defiance (novella

Kidnapped For A Day (Short Story)

THE BROTHERS OF MAYHEM SERIES

Hidden Heat

Full Heat

Naked Heat

THE SOUTHERN CRIME FAMILY

Jake

Sen (coming soon)

Ethan (coming later)

ATLANTA EDGE HOCKEY ROMANCE

Crossing The Line

Fake Play

(more to come)

SMALL-TOWN DUO

Loving The Small-Town Preacher's Son

Loving The Small-Town Hero

VAMPIRE ROMANCE

Savage Champion